Brian Sears is a trained teacher wi
primary education. He was head teacher at Yorke Mead School, Croxley
Green, Hertfordshire from 1980 until his early retirement in 1997 and
now continues teaching in one-to-one private tuition.

In 1984 Brian had six stories published by the National Christian
Education Council in an anthology, A Yearful of Stories, and has
contributed to the Scripture Union Bible reading notes, Snapshots, for
primary-school-aged children. For the last eleven football seasons Brian
has realised his other passion in that he has written a weekly column
in The Independent based on statistics of Premiership football. Eight
years ago, SU and CPO jointly published Brian's record of Christians
working in the football industry, Goal! Winning, Losing and Life,
the writing of which involved Brian in meeting the likes of Cyrille Regis,
and a memorable visit to Old Trafford to interview Manchester United's
secretary and chaplain.

Brian frequently leads church services by invitation in Hertfordshire,
mainly in the Baptist tradition. He is an enthusiastic Watford FC
supporter, two highlights being the play-off victory eleven years ago at
Wembley and telling a story about Timothy Bear at the club's annual
carol service. Brian has published two books about Timothy Bear for
Barnabas: Through the Year with Timothy Bear (2006) and Looking
Forward to Christmas with Timothy Bear (2009), in which many of
these stories first appeared, for use in school assemblies.

Text copyright © Brian Sears 2010
Illustrations copyright © Maria Maddocks 2010
The author asserts the moral right
to be identified as the author of this work

Published by
The Bible Reading Fellowship
15 The Chambers, Vineyard
Abingdon OX14 3FE
United Kingdom
Tel: +44 (0)1865 319700
Email: enquiries@brf.org.uk
Website: www.brf.org.uk
BRF is a Registered Charity

ISBN 978 1 84101 678 8

First published 2010
10 9 8 7 6 5 4 3 2 1 0
All rights reserved

Acknowledgments
Unless otherwise stated, scripture quotations are taken from the Contemporary English Version
of the Bible published by HarperCollins Publishers, copyright © 1991, 1992, 1995 American
Bible Society.

A catalogue record for this book is available from the British Library

Printed in Singapore by Craft Print International Ltd

Countdown to Christmas
with
Timothy Bear

24 five-minute read-aloud bedtime stories
for Advent

Brian Sears

To the three ladies in my life:
my wife, Ros,
and our daughters, Jennifer and Katherine.

Acknowledgments

My thanks to the staff and children of Yorke Mead School, Croxley Green, who over the years encouraged my first attempts to tell these stories. The nativity play background in so many of the stories is based on the play that Joan Hardwidge produced. Thanks also to Cassiobury School, Watford (where I was a founder pupil in 1951), Little Green School, Croxley Green (where I began my teaching career in 1967), and Mrs Chris Luddington, who has had connections with all three schools and has added many helpful suggestions.

Preface: The world of Timothy Bear

Timothy Bear's world consists mainly of his home, his school and his church. Mr and Mrs Bear are loving parents who seek the very best for Timothy and his sister Teresa. Teresa is generally most helpful to her brother but on occasions she can be a pain, as he can be to her. Grandma and Grandpa are very important figures in Timothy's and Teresa's lives. It's probably true to say that Grandpa is the last person on earth that Timothy would want to upset.

Timothy Bear attends the local primary school that takes children and bears from nursery until it's time to move on to secondary school. To begin with, Timothy was in Mrs Fletcher's class (where Teresa now is) but has now progressed to Miss Read's. Miss Read is a big influence and she's a good teacher. Miss Bridge is the head teacher. If Timothy has a best friend—he tries to be friendly with most—it's Claude. They can clash at times but they never fall out for long.

Timothy's family attend their local church and Timothy enjoys his time there. He learns about a God who is interested in everything about him; he learns about Jesus, who shows us what God is like; and he learns about the Bible, which is a book full of wonderful stories. Gradually the happenings in his life are helping him to understand where this all fits in, not only at church times but also at school, at home and in the whole of Timothy Bear's world.

Contents

— Introduction —

The Christmas story

Luke's Gospel

About that time Emperor Augustus gave orders for the names of all the people to be listed in record books. These first records were made when Quirinius was governor of Syria.

Everyone had to go to their own home town to be listed. So Joseph had to leave Nazareth in Galilee and go to Bethlehem in Judea. Long ago Bethlehem had been King David's home town, and Joseph went there because he was from David's family.

Mary was engaged to Joseph and travelled with him to Bethlehem. She was soon going to have a baby, and while they were there, she gave birth to her firstborn son. She dressed him in baby clothes and laid him on a bed of hay, because there was no room for them in the inn.

That night in the fields near Bethlehem some shepherds were guarding their sheep. All at once an angel came down to them from the Lord, and the brightness of the Lord's glory flashed around them. The shepherds were frightened. But the angel said, 'Don't be afraid! I have good news for you, which will make everyone happy. This very day in King David's home town a Saviour was born for you. He is Christ the Lord. You will know who he is, because you will find him dressed in baby clothes and lying on a bed of hay.'

Suddenly many other angels came down from heaven and joined in praising God. They said: 'Praise God in heaven! Peace on earth to everyone who pleases God.' After the angels had left and gone back to heaven, the shepherds said to each other, 'Let's go to Bethlehem and see what the Lord has told us about.' They hurried off and found Mary and Joseph, and they saw the baby lying on a bed of hay.

When the shepherds saw Jesus, they told his parents what the angel had said about him. Everyone listened and was surprised. But Mary kept thinking about all this and wondering what it meant.

As the shepherds returned to their sheep, they were praising God and saying wonderful things about him. Everything they had seen and heard was just as the angel had said.

LUKE 2:1–20

Matthew's Gospel

This is how Jesus Christ was born. A young woman named Mary was engaged to Joseph from King David's family. But before they were married, she learnt that she was going to have a baby by God's Holy Spirit. Joseph was a good man and did not want to embarrass Mary in front of everyone. So he decided to call off the wedding quietly.

While Joseph was thinking about this, an angel from the Lord came to him in a dream. The angel said, 'Joseph, the baby that Mary will have is from the Holy Spirit. Go ahead and marry her. Then after her baby is born, name him Jesus, because he will save his people from their sins.'

So the Lord's promise came true, just as the prophet had said, 'A virgin will have a baby boy, and he will be called Immanuel,' which means 'God is with us.' After Joseph woke up, he and Mary were soon married, just as the Lord's angel had told him to do. But they did not sleep together before her baby was born. Then Joseph named him Jesus.

When Jesus was born in the village of Bethlehem in Judea, Herod was king. During this time some wise men from the east came to Jerusalem and said, 'Where is the child born to be king of the Jews? We saw his star in the east and have come to worship him.'

When King Herod heard about this, he was worried, and so was everyone else in Jerusalem. Herod brought together the chief priests and the teachers of the Law of Moses and asked them, 'Where will the Messiah be born?'

They told him, 'He will be born in Bethlehem, just as the prophet wrote, "Bethlehem in the land of Judea, you are very important among the towns of Judea. From your town will come a leader, who will be like a shepherd for my people Israel."' Herod secretly called in the wise men and asked them when they had first seen the star. He told them, 'Go to Bethlehem and search carefully for the child. As soon as you find him, let me know. I want to go and worship him too.'

The wise men listened to what the king said and then left. And the star they had seen in the east went on ahead of them until it stopped over the place where the child was. They were thrilled and excited to see the star.

When the men went into the house and saw the child with Mary, his mother, they knelt down and worshipped him. They took out their gifts of gold, frankincense, and myrrh and gave them to him. Later they were warned in a dream not to return to Herod, and they went back home by another road.

MATTHEW 1:18—2:12

The wonder of Christmas

Our imaginations are a wonderful gift from God, and this book encourages us to use our imaginations as we count down through the days of Advent and think about the story of the first Christmas. The stories make ideal bedtime reading during Advent, either as a shared read-aloud experience or for older children to read for themselves. Each story is accompanied by a thought-provoking

Advent activity, designed to tease out the theme of the story, and a simple bedtime prayer.

The Christmas story is given to us quite briefly in the pages of the Bible. It is set out in just four chapters: the first two chapters of Luke and the first two chapters of Matthew. It is a story full of wonder, to set our imaginations working overtime.

Imagine Mary meeting the angel Gabriel (Luke 1:26–38). We are not told what she was actually doing just before the angel arrived. In Timothy Bear's nativity play we imagine Mary sweeping her floor. She drops her broom in surprise. What else could she have been doing? Feeding chickens? Daydreaming? The conversation with Gabriel is set down clearly for us but the surrounding circumstances are left for us to wonder about.

Timothy Bear appears to have a very strong imagination. In five stories he wonders so hard that he goes on fantastic journeys back to the first Christmas. Four times he ends up inside the stable at Bethlehem. First of all, he goes directly to the stable and meets the innkeeper's boy. That meeting comes to its end when Timothy hears the sound of the approaching donkey. All we are told in Luke 2:5 is that Mary travelled with Joseph to Bethlehem. No donkey is mentioned. Luke 2:7 tells us that Mary dressed Jesus in baby clothes and laid him on a bed of hay because there was no room for them in the inn. There's no direct mention of an innkeeper and certainly nothing about the innkeeper's boy.

Timothy often wonders about the involvement of animals in the Christmas story. He knows that the shepherds had sheep to look after (Luke 2:8–20). He imagines other animals in the stable and he imagines the wise men travelling by camel. A careful reading, however, of Matthew 2:1–12 does not mention a single camel, and certainly not the 'smallest camel' on the Christmas card that the Bear family received.

Our imaginations are not given to us just for our own enjoyment. Especially at Christmas time we should consider our giving as well as our receiving. Timothy Bear is often prompted to think of others and to share. He gives away the chocolates from his Advent calendar; he tidies up his messy bedroom; he widens his circle of friendships and is generous to his best friend, Claude; he helps his neighbour, Mrs Centurion, to be reunited with her cat, Marmalade. These are just a few of the ways Timothy helps others as they approach Christmas. There are many such opportunities for all of us.

Advent, leading up to Christmas, is truly a wonderful time. It's a time to exercise our imaginations, using the Bible story of the first Christmas as our launching pad. This book tries to do just that. Now it's over to you. I wonder...

— Day 1 —

Gruel and chocolate

… in which Timothy Bear learns a little about a boy called Oliver and what he had to eat. Timothy makes an Advent resolution to fight his flab and is tempted to break it the very next morning.

It was getting to the end of November. Timothy already knew that Christmas comes in December. The adverts on television had been talking about Christmas for some time and the decorations were already up in the shopping centre. Mrs Bear was even working on her Christmas card list. Christmas had just been mentioned at school when Miss Read started to talk to Timothy's class about putting on a special play for Christmas. First of all, however, the older children in the school were performing a play about a boy called Oliver.

'Today is the day we see the Oliver play,' announced Timothy Bear at breakfast. He was learning to remember things, especially things that sounded exciting.

'That's good,' said Dad. 'A treat for the end of November and then tomorrow starts December.'

Timothy knew bits about Oliver already. Miss Read had told her class that the boy's full name was Oliver Twist and he was an orphan. He had to live with other children who had no one to look after them, in an orphanage.

'Look out,' said Miss Read, 'for the bossy head of the orphanage, and look out for the main food served to the children. It's a weak mixture of porridge that looks a bit like pale gravy and is called gruel.' Some of the class giggled and some just shivered at the thought of it. Miss Read was setting the scene for the beginning of the play.

The play started in the orphanage with the children queuing up for their dinner. Dinner was a bowl full of that gruel. 'What a word!' thought Timothy. 'Cruel, gruel; cruel gruel.' Timothy enjoys the sounds of words but he didn't think he would enjoy the taste of gruel.

The Key Stage Two choir beautifully sang a song called 'Food, glorious food'. It was a song that imagined lots of tasty foods to compare with the gruel on offer in the orphanage. Timothy Bear's imagination ran riot with the song. 'Cold jelly and custard…' and Mrs Bear's honey crumble and ice cream. 'Pease pudding and savelopys'—Timothy had his doubts about those from the song but not about his mum's roast turkey and stuffing. 'Just picture a great big steak; just picture some Christmas cake…' He could dream about all the Christmas treats that awaited him, dreams that would become real. Mrs Bear is a good cook all year long but she excels herself at Christmas.

Timothy rubbed his tummy in anticipation—a tummy that bulged a bit too much already. Mum had already mentioned that he shouldn't become too tubby.

By this time, the gruel meal was almost over in the orphanage. The time had come for Oliver to stand up and move forward towards the Year 6 boy playing the part of the large man who was in charge.

'Please, sir,' asked Oliver most politely, 'I want some more.'

How hungry he must be to want more of that gruel— more of that slimy mush!

'More?!' exploded the large man.

Timothy Bear was left wondering if some people were still around who existed on drab food like gruel. He certainly didn't, and he thought again about his tubby tummy and his need to do something about it. Then it suddenly hit him. To get ready for the delights of Christmas, he would give up sweets and honey until Christmas came. He really would.

Having made his resolution, Timothy enjoyed the rest of the Oliver play. He could understand about Oliver becoming a pickpocket. He wasn't sure what to make of the old man called Fagin, though. He preferred his grandpa! It was a great story and so well performed. He was full of it at home that evening. Mrs Bear, too, had something to tell him.

'Have you remembered, Timothy, that December starts tomorrow? We have something for you—one for you and one for Teresa.'

Timothy had completely forgotten that it was time for Advent calendars.

'These were the only ones left in the shop,' confessed Mrs Bear. 'They have a wrapped chocolate surprise behind each picture.'

'Oh no!' sighed Timothy, paw going to his mouth. 'I've given up sweets till Christmas.' He explained what he had decided during the play at school.

'Good,' said Mrs Bear. You can keep the chocolates in Grandma's tin until you decide what to do with them.'

What a good idea! But it was hard when Timothy got up the next morning and opened the first window of the calendar.

'Mine's a donkey,' he said, very pleased. The chocolate was in his paw.

'Mine's a star,' said his sister, unwrapping the chocolate and popping it in her mouth. She was lucky to have no worries about her weight.

It was very hard for Timothy not to unwrap his chocolate. Mum produced Grandma's tin and smiled encouragement as Timothy popped the chocolate in the tin instead of his mouth. He'd already had his favourite cereal for breakfast and didn't feel hungry at all.

'How things have changed since the days of Oliver Twist,' thought Timothy to himself.

Advent activity

Resolutions are usually made at the start of a new year, but is there an Advent resolution for you to make in the countdown to Christmas?

Prayer

Dear Lord Jesus, Advent is all about getting ready for your coming into the world. Help us to celebrate the joy of your birth each day this Advent. Amen

— Day 2 —

Timothy Bear and the innkeeper's boy

… in which Timothy Bear goes on an amazing journey and meets a boy who is getting ready for the first Christmas. Timothy makes up his mind to prepare properly for this Christmas.

Timothy Bear usually gets excited about Christmas so early that it makes him careless, and this year was no exception.

'Your bedroom's a mess,' said Mrs Bear. 'Yesterday I tripped on a marble and had to put your toys away again.'

Timothy was forgetting his pleases and thank-yous as well. At school, it was his paw-writing and his colouring that were going wrong.

'It's all so messy,' sighed Miss Read.

In fact, it was his carelessness that found Timothy in the school hall all on his own. He'd taken a photograph to show in assembly and had left it on the floor. Miss Read had said he could go and fetch it.

Timothy was surprised at how dark it was in the hall, but then he remembered that the curtains were drawn so that they could start rehearsing this year's nativity play later in the day. Already the stage blocks were out and a roll of corrugated paper was showing the walls of a stable. The door that swung on hinges had been much admired in assembly. Miss Read and the other teachers were good at this kind of thing.

Miss Read was promising to give out the parts for the play that morning. Timothy had been a shepherd in last year's play. As he thought about it, somehow he felt drawn to the stable and sat for a moment on the stage block by the door. Whether it was the darkness or the empty hall, Timothy didn't know, but suddenly he seemed to be floating through time and space—spinning but never dizzy, speeding but never frightened—and he landed with the slightest bump.

Timothy was still in a stable, but a real stable—a real stable with a real smell, and in the darkness he could make out the shape of a boy. The boy was wearing a short-sleeved robe and was working hard. He was working around Timothy Bear, sweeping, putting things straight and tidying. Timothy coughed nervously. The boy turned and smiled as if he expected to see him.

'Hello, Tubby!'

'Well!' thought Timothy, but he said, 'Good morning. Who are you?'

'My dad's the innkeeper and I'm doing some tidying up.'

'You're doing it very well,' said Timothy. 'I'm not very tidy,' he added.

'No, I'm not really,' went on the boy, 'but there's a feeling of something special in the air. I'm sure something special is going to happen, and I want to be ready for it.'

'Where are we?' Timothy wanted to know.

'This is Bethlehem,' said the boy. 'It's not an important place, but crowds of people are coming to fill in their census forms. The stars seem so bright and this stable of ours seems so still, as if it's waiting for something to happen.'

Timothy nodded. He was beginning to understand, but the boy was speaking again.

'It's not like me, but I want to be ready. I want it to look nice, smell nice. I've blocked up some of the draughts and I've tried to mend the door. I'm really pleased.'

Timothy opened his mouth but nothing came out. He wanted to say, 'Yes, you're right. Something special is about to happen.' But he only nodded.

Again the boy was talking. 'I feel so much better. I haven't enjoyed tidying up before, but this is different.'

Again Timothy's words wouldn't come out. He wanted to say, 'You're getting ready for a very special baby. He'll make all the difference in the world.' Instead, the boy said, 'What's that noise?'

This time Timothy did speak. 'It sounds like a donkey.'

Timothy was feeling that strange sensation again of floating through time and space—spinning but never dizzy, speeding but never frightened—and he landed with the slightest bump. He was on the stage block in his school hall. He picked up the photograph and returned to his classroom.

The innkeeper's boy was on his mind. Yes, Timothy decided, he would really get ready for Christmas as well this year. He'd get ready carefully and tidily. If the innkeeper's boy could do it, so could he.

Advent activity

Think of a place that is yours to tidy up. Ask if you are allowed to do it.

Prayer

Dear Lord Jesus, help us to be ready in every way we can when Christmas comes. Amen

★

— Day 3 —

The cloak and the crown

… in which Miss Read has a very difficult task as a teacher, Timothy Bear is disappointed and then saves the day for Claude.

Miss Read made the announcement to her class immediately after assembly.

'We're going to do a play for Christmas. Its main part will be about the birth of baby Jesus. It is called a nativity play.'

Timothy Bear's class were listening very hard indeed. You might say they were all ears! They like learning new words, and 'nativity' sounded a good new word. Timothy Bear had actually heard the word before. He had been part of his church's nativity play the year before. He had been the wise man who presented baby Jesus with gold. He still had the long flowing cloak Mrs Bear had made for him and the shiny gold crown they had made together.

Miss Read looked round at all the bright, upturned faces of her class. She knew it would be one of the hardest things of all, to announce who she had decided would play the main parts in the play. Most of her class were keen to be actors.

'We will need lots of you to join the rest of the school as the children of Bethlehem. You will be our choir,' she said. 'But there are some particular parts to be taken in the play. Amanda, I wonder if you will be Mary the mother of Jesus.'

Amanda went pink with pleasure and nodded several times.

'And Paul,' went on Miss Read, 'you should be a good Joseph as you're good at making things.'

Paul was as surprised as the rest of the class that he had been chosen. He was not always the best behaved, but now he, too, nodded his head.

Miss Read went on to suggest children to be angels and shepherds, narrators and the innkeeper. Timothy Bear's name had not yet been mentioned. He didn't mind as he'd set his heart on being a wise man again. After all, he did have the cloak and the crown, and so many had said at church what a fine wise man he had made. He would like his gift to be the gold again, but he'd make do with the frankincense or the myrrh.

'That leaves the parts of the three wise men,' continued Miss Read. 'Claude, I'd like you to bring the gold; David, you to bring the frankincense; and Michael to look after the myrrh.'

Miss Read caught sight of Timothy Bear's earnest face covered with disappointment and it rang a bell in her memory.

'Oh, and Timothy Bear, I want you to be the innkeeper's boy. Do you think a teddy bear can play the part of a boy?'

Timothy managed a watery smile. He felt a bit tearful but he nodded. It certainly wasn't the part he wanted. He had no idea what part an innkeeper's boy would play. But Claude had his hand up. Miss Read looked enquiringly in Claude's direction.

'I'd like to be a wise man,' said Claude quietly, 'but I don't think my mum will let me. We're having an extension built at home, and Mum's so busy, she won't have time to get me ready.'

'That is a problem, Claude,' replied Miss Read. 'We have to ask parents to see to the costumes and things like that. Yes, Timothy?'

Miss Read had spotted Timothy with his paw in the air. Perhaps he would volunteer to take Claude's place. She had wondered about Timothy being a wise man.

'I already have a cloak and a crown,' began Timothy. 'I'm sure Claude can have them.'

Miss Read clapped her hands together. Claude's face lit up with delight. He would be able to be the wise man who brings gold to Jesus, after all.

'Well done, Timothy,' exclaimed Miss Read. 'If we're all as helpful as you, this will indeed be a Christmas play to remember.'

Advent activity

Can you think of a time when, like Timothy, you have been disappointed? Perhaps you can find someone to talk to about it. Do you know someone who has been chosen to do something special? Can you help them to do it even better?

Prayer

Sometimes, what we would like to happen doesn't happen. Help us then, Lord Jesus, to be brave and to go on thinking of others. Amen

★

Broom-dropping moments

… in which Mary is greatly surprised by a visit from an angel. Timothy has a surprise meeting with a robin and rescues Marmalade, and Mrs Centurion reckons Timothy to be an angel himself.

Amanda was very good at playing the part of Mary, right from the first rehearsal. Even before she had her costume, she entered into the part so well that the rest of the class forgot it was Amanda and really thought she was the young girl, Mary, living two thousand years ago.

The first scene began with Mary in her little home in Nazareth. She was looking after things—feeding the chickens, tidying up—and then she would take hold of a broom to sweep the floor. The audience would clearly see the angel appearing on the stage before Mary realised he was there. After all, Mary was looking down at the floor.

Mary stopped sweeping as if something had disturbed her. She looked up and she, too, saw the angel. You could see the surprise on Mary's face and her broom went crashing to the floor.

'It's a broom-dropping moment,' thought Timothy to himself as he watched from the side of the stage.

Moments later, Mary had been told she was to have a baby boy, God's Son, and she said, 'Yes, I understand. I am God's servant. Let it happen as you say.'

It was some opening scene, and Miss Read was thrilled with the way things were going. Amanda had been a very good choice. Timothy Bear thought it was a great start, too. What drama! To meet an angel! An angel with such a message! A broom-dropping moment, indeed!

The next Saturday, Timothy woke up and immediately felt strangely excited. There was a pale glow on his bedroom ceiling. He felt drawn to his window and, sure enough, he looked out on to a white world. Snow had fallen gently in the night. There was no thought now of getting back into bed. He launched himself into Mr and Mrs Bear's room.

'It's been snowing,' he gasped, waking them up. 'Please! May I get dressed and go outside?'

Mr Bear was nodding his head.

'Two jumpers, your woolly hat and boots,' said Mum.

'You might even clear the path for us,' added Dad. 'I put the broom in the porch last night, just in case, when I saw the forecast.'

'Certainly!' shouted Timothy, already halfway down the stairs.

What a morning it was! It was still so early that cars had not yet disturbed the snow in the road. Trees and shrubs looked like white umbrellas. The world was so still and so quiet. Timothy held the broom to clear the path. Then something made him look up. It was something on the whiter-than-white lawn. It was a robin. The red breast looked brighter than usual in this white world. The robin was so close to Timothy, closer than any bird had ever been before. The surprise made Timothy drop the broom. Fortunately the snow muffled the sound of the falling broom and the robin was not put off at all. Bear and robin looked comfortably at each other and Timothy realised that the robin must be hungry. The usual food supplies for birds were buried under centimetres of snow.

'I won't be long,' whispered Timothy.

Timothy had no doubt that the robin would be there on his return, and he was right. Timothy came back with a plate of breadcrumbs and a small beaker of water. He wasn't sure if birds knew they could get water from snow.

Timothy cleared the path, glancing across every so often at the robin having breakfast.

'It's another broom-dropping moment,' thought Timothy to himself, 'but I didn't expect them to happen to me.'

It wasn't quite all over. Path cleared and breakfast eaten, the robin hadn't finished with Timothy yet. Three or four times it hopped backwards and forwards over the fence into Mrs Centurion's garden. At last Timothy got the message that he should go round as well. Perhaps it would be a good idea to clear Mrs Centurion's path. But the robin led the way through the open gate into Mrs Centurion's back garden. The robin would go no further, but by now Timothy could hear a soft miaowing coming from the shed at the end of the garden. Mrs Centurion's cat, Marmalade, must be trapped inside.

Timothy Bear went to Marmalade's rescue. Somehow the door of the shed had closed on Marmalade the evening before and she had been imprisoned. She was only too willing to be cradled in Timothy's paws after he pulled open the door. Bear and cat made their way to the back door. Mrs Centurion came to the door in her dressing-gown. Her worried face broke into smiles as she was reunited with Marmalade.

'I was just wondering what had happened to her,' she said. 'Timothy Bear, you're an angel.'

If Timothy had been holding his broom, he would have dropped it! An angel! He modestly looked round to give the robin the credit, but the robin had flown away.

Advent activity

Talk with family members or friends about any 'broom-dropping' moments that you've had—times when you've thought, 'Wow! That's wonderful.'

Prayer

Dear God, thank you that you always care for us and continually show us your presence in the world. Help us to see you in our daily lives as we get ready for Christmas. Amen

— Day 5 —

The expert at making heads

… in which Timothy at last gets his snowy wish, Grandma visits, and Mum recalls an old skill from the days when she was young.

Timothy Bear hasn't known many days of snow in his young life. He often wishes it would snow—the kind of snow that settles and lasts. Somehow his wishes don't seem strong enough, though—nowhere near as strong as Mrs Bear's wishes must be.

'I only hope it doesn't snow,' says Mum when the temperature falls and the clouds roll in. 'It's the last thing we need.'

At last Timothy had his wish, and on a Saturday, too. The snow was quite deep even before breakfast. When Timothy made a snowball, it held together well and he even hit the gatepost with his first throw. At breakfast Mum certainly was not sharing Timothy's excitement.

'It's so cold,' she moaned, 'and my house will get

pawprints all over it. What weather!' Mum went on in her moaning voice.

'What weather!' thought Timothy to himself in quite a different kind of voice.

Mr Bear and Teresa were getting ready to go out.

'We're picking up Grandma from the station,' announced Dad. 'The snow's not too deep for that.'

Timothy had completely forgotten that Grandma was coming for the weekend. Life couldn't be better, thought Timothy. Snow and Grandma both staying!

As Mrs Bear started making tea, Grandma dressed in her outdoor clothes. 'You're not going, Grandma?' asked Timothy.

'No,' answered Grandma, glancing at Mrs Bear. 'I'm taking my grandcub out in the garden to build a snowbear. Get your warm clothes on, Timothy.'

That's what Timothy liked about Grandma—she was always full of lovely surprises.

'Ridiculous,' said Mrs Bear. 'You two are as bad as each other.'

The snow was just right for building, and the snowbear grew quickly. It was going to be as tall as Timothy. Timothy and Grandma rolled a large snowball for the head, but when they put it in place it didn't look right at all. When they tried to improve it, they only seemed to make it worse.

'Your mum was the expert at heads when she was your age,' said Grandma at last. 'I wonder if she'd give us some help now.'

★

'I'll ask her,' said Timothy, sliding through the snow to the kitchen door. 'We need help with the snowbear's head,' blurted out Timothy to Mrs Bear, who had her hands in a bowl of flour. 'Grandma says you're the expert.'

'What nonsense!' said Mrs Bear. 'Make a snowbear, at my age? What about tea? Do you want us all to starve?'

Then she stopped. In her mind's eye she was seeing herself as a young bear in her bobble hat as everyone admired her snowbear with its life-like head. She reached for her red scarf and red bobble hat.

'Well, I suppose, if you really can't manage it, I can spare five minutes.'

When Mr Bear came down from working on the computer with Teresa, he declared the snowbear to be the best he'd ever seen—especially with the red scarf and bobble hat round its splendid head. Timothy sat in the warm glow of the fire with the curtains drawn back. Hot tea, potatoes in their jackets and Grandma here to stay!

When it was bedtime, he went over to the window. It was still snowing, and the snowbear stood firmly in the garden as if he was staying for at least a week.

'What weather, what brilliant weather,' murmured Timothy Bear, and behind him Mrs Bear winked at the snowbear.

Advent activity

Can you make a picture of the snowbear that Timothy made with his grandma and his mum? You may want to use white crayons or cut out white paper on a very dark background.

Prayer

Dear Lord Jesus, help all those who are getting so busy at this Advent time. Help them to have times when they can relax and not be too stressed. Amen

— Day 6 —

The toy service

... in which we meet Auntie Katherine, Timothy loses his pencil sharpener and finds it again, fills up his shoebox and tells Auntie Katherine a secret.

Timothy Bear likes his Auntie Katherine. She's funny and serious, noisy and quiet, daft and clever. He always enjoys her visits. Timothy can just remember the time when she wasn't around. When she was working in Egypt, letters had come with foreign stamps on them; there had been phone calls and emails. Eventually Auntie Katherine came back with tales of pyramids, great big statues and trips up and down an enormous river, but most of all with stories of garbage village children.

She still spends part of her life, now she is back in her own country, working to provide help for those children in Egypt. That was why she came to speak at Timothy's church the week before the toy service. The church always has a toy service as part of the countdown to Christmas, and that year Auntie Katherine's Egyptian charity was to be given the toys and the money collected. The toys were going to be fitted into shoeboxes and given as presents to children living in those garbage villages. Timothy was delighted. It would mean Auntie Katherine visiting them two or three weekends running.

'They're called garbage villages,' Auntie Katherine explained when she spoke in church, 'because the homes are near to huge rubbish dumps. The children help their parents sort through everyone else's waste to find items that can be recycled or are still useful.' Auntie Katherine went on to explain how the families had little money with which to celebrate Christmas, and not much at all for buying presents.

'In this country, we can help,' went on Auntie Katherine. 'I can make sure all your gifts get to a church that will share them out among the poorest children.' Auntie Katherine promised to come back the next week for the toy service. 'There's a family here that put me up and put up with me,' she smiled, giving Timothy and Teresa a great big wink.

At the beginning of the week, Timothy began to think about what he could spare from his toys. There was that old pencil with the broken lead that he'd found down the side of a chair, a tractor with a wobbly wheel, and a book he'd finished. He started collecting the items in a shoebox that Mrs Bear had found in the attic.

Then, on Tuesday, Timothy remembered what Auntie Katherine had said about how poor some of the children were. Timothy felt ashamed of his growing collection. They were mostly broken toys or things he could easily throw out.

The drawers and cupboards of his room were bulging with his possessions. He was rich! He replaced the tractor with a car that sped across the carpet, he removed the old book and added one about the football Premier League, and he put in a brand new set of colouring crayons instead of the broken pencil.

On Thursday night, Timothy couldn't find his favourite pencil sharpener. It was silver and in the shape of a honey pot. He searched his desk and his room but it was nowhere to be seen. Mum asked her usual question about lost things: 'Where did you have it last?'

Timothy thought hard. It must have been when he last sharpened pencils over his wastepaper basket. That would be it! But when he investigated, the basket was empty. Dad had done his clearing up as thoroughly as usual.

'Perhaps it's in the black sack in the wheelie bin in the garden,' suggested Dad when Timothy explained his problem. Timothy continued the hunt. He climbed up on to the garden seat and lifted the lid of the wheelie bin. Fortunately there was an outside light in the garden, so Timothy could see, but he shivered in the cold. The smell was dreadful! His paws explored the mixture within the black sack—sometimes slimy, sometimes sharp.

At that moment, Timothy remembered the children in Egypt, searching rubbish regularly—searching the rubbish of other families, not even their own. At last Timothy felt the smooth shape of a honey pot and pulled out the missing pencil sharpener. It was a very thoughtful Timothy who went back indoors.

By Sunday, Timothy had a shoebox packed with his belongings—real treasures. There was a special part of the toy service when, as the congregation sang carols, everyone took their gifts to the front and handed them to Auntie Katherine in person. It so happened that Timothy was last in line. Auntie Katherine smiled at him. She realised how generous Timothy was being in the gifts he was giving, but she was in for an extra surprise. Timothy held on to his box a little longer to whisper something in Auntie Katherine's ear.

'I've got a secret,' Timothy murmured seriously. 'When I'm old enough, I want to go to Egypt to help those children myself.'

Auntie Katherine smiled again, but this time a lump was forming in her throat and her smile became a little watery.

Advent activity

There may be ways in which you can find out about the needs of a particular country in our world. There may be things you can do to meet some of those needs.

Prayer

We know, O God, that you love the whole world, so we bring those parts of it that are on our minds to you. We remember street children and children who must search through rubbish. Amen

★

First light

... in which the shepherds fidget, Timothy remembers a morning of his summer holidays, and his brainwave calms down the shepherds.

Miss Read was having trouble with the shepherds. She had chosen five children who she thought would make good shepherds but, as it turned out, they were not good at waiting patiently. They were such fidgets. They even picked away at the green plastic grass on which they sat, and they couldn't control their crooks properly. The result was that when the extra lights suddenly came on with the appearance of the angels, the shepherds were all over the place and in no way ready to look amazed and awestruck.

'I don't know what I'm going to do with you shepherds,' complained Miss Read at the third rehearsal. 'Why can't you be more like proper shepherds?'

'What about giving us thick sticks so we can fight off wild animals?' wondered Josh, who had a thing about weapons.

'You have enough trouble looking after your crooks,' pointed out Miss Read.

'Shepherds were skilled with their slings, too,' went on Josh.

Miss Read shook her head firmly. 'We're certainly not going to risk you shepherds having stones to sling around.'

Even the shepherds had to agree with Miss Read about that.

But Timothy Bear was in the middle of a brainwave. He would tell Miss Read about it at playtime. Timothy was remembering a wonderful day in their family holiday by the sea. Mr Bear had challenged Timothy to go with him on an early morning walk to the next bay along from the one where their caravan was parked. Timothy had been delighted.

Father and cub were up before sunrise. The sun actually appeared on the horizon as they began their walk. Nature, too, seemed to be waking up around them. A rabbit peeped at Timothy over the cliff top. Sunrise was awesome, spine-tingling. It made your fur stand on end.

When they reached the bay, it was a huge pebble beach.

'There must be millions of pebbles,' thought Timothy. 'Perhaps billions.'

Mr Bear and Timothy crunched their way back towards their bay. One pebble caught Timothy's eye. He had never seen one quite like it before. It was the shape of a giant polo mint or a small doughnut with a hole right through its middle. Timothy picked it up.

'Keep that in your pocket,' said Mr Bear. 'I've got an idea it will come in useful later this morning, when we go to the quay where the boats come in.'

Timothy didn't understand what his father was up to, but knew him well enough to look forward to the surprise to come. While they were getting breakfast ready, Timothy noticed Mr Bear putting the rind from the bacon into a plastic bag. He also put a ball of string in with it.

'Don't forget your special pebble,' said Mr Bear to Timothy as the family left for the quayside. 'And we must stop at the shop and buy the biggest bucket they've got.'

Half an hour later, the whole family were enjoying Mr Bear's secret. It was a crabbing expedition. Timothy and Teresa sat next to each other on the quayside. The string was dangling over the edge between them, weighted down by Timothy's special stone. The bacon rind was tied to the other end of the string, deep down in the water. Every so often, Timothy and Teresa would feel tugs and tremors on the string and, with great patience, would reel it in to find a crab helping itself to a bacon breakfast. In all, they caught 13 crabs in their bucket. When it was time to go, Timothy tossed them all back into their watery home. 'What a wonderful, wonderful morning,' Timothy had thought.

During the rest of the holiday, Timothy had made a collection of stones with holes through them. He still had them at home. Now, the problem with the shepherds at school had brought those stones to Timothy's mind. What if Miss Read tied one of his stones firmly and safely to the string of each sling so that the shepherds could pretend to fire them at wild animals?

At playtime, Miss Read listened to Timothy's plan and then had an idea of her own. The shepherds could have special stones made from pompoms, which would look realistic without causing any danger of injury. When she mentioned it to the shepherds, they were intrigued. What a trick it would be when all their parents were sitting in the audience!

'But,' pointed out Miss Read, 'it will all depend on how well you practise the rest of the play. If you're always ready to be shocked and amazed when the dazzling angels light up the stage, then we'll see about making special stones for the actual performances.'

The shepherds were transformed. At every rehearsal from then on, they were the best-behaved shepherds the school had ever known.

Advent activity

Remember together some special holidays that you have enjoyed and places you have visited. You might be able to find those places on a map.

Prayer

Dear Lord Jesus, thank you for the wonderful world you have made for us. We thank you for unexpected things, like holes going right through stones. Amen

— Day 8 —

Linda the lights

... in which spotlights are loaned to the school for their play, Linda is given her part, and goes on to star without being on the stage at all.

Miss Read was worried about Linda in her class. She was so shy and so quiet; she hardly said a word, even when some children made fun of her for being so quiet. Amanda was often the ringleader in the teasing but sometimes Timothy Bear joined in, poking fun. Even then, Linda just looked sad and said nothing. Mrs Fletcher told Miss Read it had been the same when Linda was in her class. Mrs Fletcher had discussed it with Linda's mum.

'She's quiet at home as well,' her mum had agreed, 'but she notices things and she's brilliant at finding lost things. "Linda the light" we call her.'

Miss Read had no idea what Linda could do in the nativity play—until a friend of the school whom they called Mr Mac (he was a Scotsman whose real name was Mr Macnamara) promised to loan the school a number of spotlights to make the hall more like a theatre for Christmas plays.

'They'll need a good young operator,' pointed out Mr Mac, 'someone to switch them on and off just at the right times. They come with a board that has eight switches on it.'

Immediately Miss Read thought back to her staffroom conversation with Mrs Fletcher. 'Linda the light' could surely become 'Linda the lights'. So Linda sat at the side of the hall, script in hand, switching lights on or off at just the right moments. When the angels came on, every switch was in its 'on' position to give the brightest light possible. That was easy. But Linda's favourite moment in the play was when Mary, in the darkened stable, placed the wrapped-up baby Jesus in the feeding trough. Just at that moment, Linda would switch on the single spotlight that bathed the manger in its golden glow to indicate the presence of Jesus.

'Jesus is the light himself,' thought 'Linda the lights'.

Linda, just like her mother had said, was good at noticing things. She began to put things right as well. She spotted that Mary's broom was in the wrong place and held it out for Amanda to collect. Linda also realised when Amanda forgot what she had to say back to the angel. Linda whispered what Amanda should be saying from her script so that hardly anyone spotted that Amanda had hesitated. It didn't occur to Linda to try to get her own back for all the times Amanda had been nasty to her in the playground.

Linda noticed, too, when two of the wise men had their socks untidily about their ankles after their game of football. 'Pull your socks up,' she whispered as they were getting ready to pick up their gifts.

One afternoon, Miss Read said that they would have circle time before their rehearsal. Circle time was a chance for members of the class to talk over things that were on their minds. This afternoon Linda put her hand up to be passed the shell. When you held the shell, it was your turn to speak. Linda had never spoken in circle time before. Everyone was surprised, including Miss Read. Amanda did just wonder if Linda would tell everyone how horrid she could be. It crossed Timothy Bear's mind that he might be in trouble.

'I just think our last play rehearsal was a bit dull,' said Linda. 'We've stopped doing our best.'

'How can we improve it?' asked Miss Read. She remembered thinking that the last rehearsal had been a bit ordinary.

'Well,' continued Linda slowly, 'I'm going to imagine that someone special is watching us. For me it will be Mr Mac.'

Timothy put up his paw and was passed the shell. 'I'll pretend my mum is watching.'

Amanda put her hand up. 'I shall think of baby Jesus being alive and kicking in the manger,' she said.

Everyone smiled with pleasure.

'That's lovely,' concluded Miss Read. 'Let's go for our next rehearsal now.'

Linda noticed that Miss Read was walking more slowly than usual, and when she sat on her chair in the hall she flopped a bit and looked very pale. While everyone else was getting to their places, Linda went to Miss Bridge's room.

'I don't think Miss Read's very well,' blurted out Linda. Miss Bridge came at once and talked quietly with Miss Read. Miss Bridge clapped her hands together for all the class to listen.

'Miss Read has been so busy, she hasn't had time to eat anything all day. Linda, you see your teacher safely to the staffroom, and then I will have the treat of seeing how your play is coming along.'

So now there would be a real 'special' person watching their rehearsal as well as all the pretend ones: their head teacher would be in the hall. 'Linda the lights' took her place in front of the switches. Miss Read, eating her ham rolls and then her toffee yogurt in the staffroom, was grateful that Linda noticed so much. Miss Bridge was grateful, too, that Linda was telling people more of what she was noticing, and Amanda gave Linda her best friendly smile.

Advent activity

How many grown-ups can you think of who work in a school that you or someone in your family goes to? If you like, make a list of the names.

Prayer

We thank you, dear God, that you give all of us things that we are good at. Help us to do everything as well as we can. Amen

★

— Day 9 —

Peace on earth

… in which Timothy is having a bad day—until he thinks things through in his special place and finds peace on his part of the earth.

One of the many high points of the nativity play was when the angels had gathered to one side of the stage. A spotlight picked out Barbara Pole, who had been chosen to deliver the message to the shepherds about the wonderful birth in Bethlehem's stable. Then, as the shepherds stood spellbound, every light came fully on. Half of the angels proclaimed, 'Praise God in heaven!' and the other half added, 'Peace on earth to everyone who pleases God.' Then the whole school sang the angels' song before the shepherds were left in the dark to decide what to do.

Timothy Bear, for once at this rehearsal, did not join in with the singing in his usual wholehearted way. This day was not turning out gloriously for Timothy. He did not feel peaceful.

It had been an unsettled and unsettling day right from the start. Timothy had been slow getting ready for school—so slow that in the end he had made Mrs Bear cross. At playtime, he'd ganged up with others in his class to make fun of a girl called Alex, saying she had a boy's name. They went much too far and even made Alex cry. Fortunately for Timothy, Alex didn't mention his name to their head teacher when Miss Bridge came to sort things out, but Timothy knew he was partly to blame. There was little praise on the playground and no peace at all.

After playtime there was the nativity rehearsal, and Timothy nearly tripped Amanda up as he was leading her to the stable. For once, it put Amanda off and she was a bit flustered. Timothy went on feeling unsettled.

In the afternoon, Miss Read was out on a course, and Timothy knew he wasn't trying as hard as he could with the picture that the new teacher was asking the class to make. Praise? Peace? They were nowhere to be seen!

Hometime was not the usual joyful experience. Timothy didn't notice how busy his mum was, getting ahead with Christmas cooking.

'Timothy, could you sort out the clean clothes in the airing cupboard, please? They need to be sorted into piles for each one of us.' Why was it always him who was landed with jobs to do? Hadn't Teresa got paws as well? Timothy was too upset to notice that his paws hadn't been cleaned after his picture-making at school, so you might guess what the clothes looked like in their wobbly piles.

Just as Timothy thought he had done enough clothes

sorting, Teresa came bouncing in to ask her brother to play a game with her.

'Certainly not,' burst out Timothy. 'I'm light years ahead of you at every game on the planet.'

Timothy hadn't seen Mrs Bear standing outside the open door on the landing. She heard Timothy's loud voice, saw the crumbling face of Teresa and the messy, untidy piles of her laundry.

'Timothy,' she said in her stern voice, 'you'd better have some time out under the stairs.'

Mrs Bear and Timothy both knew that this was a signal for Timothy to sort himself out. Under the stairs was a small cupboard with enough space for Timothy to sit in it. Usually it was a favourite place, but that evening it seemed dark and dusty. There was no praise at all. What a mess he'd made of things. But what had the vicar said in church last week—about times to say sorry, times for new starts, and time for baby Jesus to grow into Jesus the Saviour and offer forgiveness?

Timothy was indeed very sorry for all he'd made go wrong. The angel had spoken to the shepherds about a Saviour in the stable. It was still dark under the stairs but it was as if a little light began to shine inside Timothy Bear, and with it came some peace. He would tell Teresa and Mrs Bear how sorry he was. Tomorrow he'd make it up with Alex as well.

The light and peace grew inside him and he remembered the words of the angels at the beginning of their song. This time, deep under the stairs, Timothy sang it out wholeheartedly: 'Praise God in heaven! Peace on earth to everyone who pleases God!'

Advent activity

When did you last feel a bit unsettled and 'down in the dumps'? Try to talk through such times together.

Prayer

Dear Lord Jesus, we are sorry about the things we do that upset us, upset others and upset you. Thank you that when we've said sorry, you set things the right way up again. Amen

★

— Day 10 —

Decorating by numbers

... in which Timothy's difficulties in maths are mentioned at school and then, at home, Christmas preparations help his maths and make a difference back at school.

It was on a Friday that Miss Read made her comment about Timothy Bear's maths.

'It's such a shame, Timothy, but your maths really lets you down. I know you do your best,' his teacher told him, 'but you could do with a maths brain or two as a Christmas present.'

Timothy reported Miss Read's comment when he was at home that evening. Mr and Mrs Bear already knew that Timothy had a few problems with his maths and his spelling.

'There's nothing we can do about your maths this weekend,' said Mum. 'It's all hands on deck tomorrow, putting up our Christmas decorations.'

'Wait a bit,' put in Dad thoughtfully. 'We might be able to kill two birds with one stone.'

'Two birds… one stone. What on earth is that all about?' asked a mystified Timothy.

'Well,' said Dad, 'let's see what tomorrow brings.'

To begin with, Saturday morning brought pouring rain— ideal weather, they all thought, for putting up decorations. Mr Bear brought the boxes of stored decorations down from the loft and Mrs Bear found all the new stuff she had been buying over the last few weeks. Teresa was given the tree to decorate. Dad took Timothy into the study. On the desk was a shape that Dad had cut from the back of a cereal packet.

'That's a triangle,' announced Timothy.

'It's a very special triangle,' pointed out Dad. 'All three sides are six centimetres long. When the sides are all the same length, it's called an equilateral triangle.'

Timothy tried to say the word for himself. He found it difficult and giggled.

Dad showed him how to draw round the triangle, then turn it upside down and draw round it again, on top of the first drawing, to make a six-pointed star.

'Do-it-yourself decorations,' chuckled Dad. 'Then add colour. While you're making stars, here's something to work out. There are 24 windows on your Advent calendar. If you have one chocolate for each day and don't eat any of them, we know how many you'd end up with—24. But how many would you end up with if you collected two chocolates each day?'

When Dad returned, Timothy had made six stars out of the rest of the cereal packet, but none of them were coloured yet.

'That chocolate sum was easy,' Timothy said. 'Miss Read is teaching us our two times table. It starts 2, 4, 6, 8, and I went on to 24 times, which is 48.'

'Well done,' nodded Dad. 'What about if it was five chocolates a day? And how many would you end up with if you collected three chocolates each day?'

Dad had more to say. 'While you're doing those sums, here's another decoration to make by drawing round that special equilateral triangle.' Dad showed Timothy a sketch of the way the triangles could be drawn to build up into a solid pyramid.

'We'll be able to hang it on our tree,' pointed out Mr Bear.

'Wow,' thought Timothy to himself when his dad had disappeared again. 'I'm enjoying this, even though it's about maths.'

Teresa appeared at the door of the study. She was bored with the Christmas tree.

'I could do with someone like you, who is good at colouring,' suggested Timothy. 'And I can teach you some maths at the same time.'

Timothy was surprised at how quickly his sister got the hang of counting in fives while she was colouring. Dad was delighted to see them both busy when he came back later. He showed Timothy how to make the pyramid decoration by folding the large equilateral triangle. Timothy promised he'd make at least one more for his sister.

'We reckon that five chocolates a day would get you 120 by the end of Advent,' said Timothy. 'Would three a day get you to 72?' he wondered.

Dad nodded. 'Now for making snowflakes,' he went on.

Dad had already cut out circles of thin paper. He showed Timothy and Teresa how to fold each one into six triangular sections and then make small cuts in the folds.

'Now unfold the circles,' said Dad. His cubs were delighted with what they discovered. They were keen to make many more.

'But only when I'm with you,' warned Mr Bear. 'You'll have to use the very sharp scissors.'

'While we've been doing this,' said Timothy, 'I've thought up a maths problem for you, Dad. I can't even work out the answer. If you gave me 1p on the first day I open my Advent calendar, 2p on the second, 4p on the third, 8p on the fourth and so on, doubling the amount each day, how much will you have given me by Christmas Eve?'

Dad smiled. 'I'll work it out, but don't expect me to give you the money. I think it might work out to more than £100.'*

By the time Monday morning arrived, the Bear household had more decorations than ever before. Their favourites were the new ones that had been paw-made over the weekend. There were stars, pyramids and snowflakes, many of them beautifully coloured.

That same Monday morning, Miss Read settled her class for number work before they rehearsed their nativity play.

'We've given enough time to the two times table,' she told them. 'Let's go on to the threes. Who thinks they can already count up in threes?'

Miss Read was surprised to see Timothy's paw up in the

air, with two or three other hands.

'You try, Timothy, please.'

Timothy started softly but then, as he remembered the imagined chocolates, his voice grew stronger. '3, 6, 9, 12, 15, 18, 21, 24, 27, 30, 33, 36, 39…'

'That's far enough,' interrupted Miss Read. 'Very well done, Timothy. I think the Christmas present I suggested on Friday has come early. Children, we have a new budding mathematician among us!'

Timothy beamed with pleasure. Maybe they had.

'And if you like,' added Timothy, 'I'll show you things you can make from equilateral triangles.' No one minded that Timothy still stuttered over that difficult 'equilateral' word.

Advent activity

Try to make some of the decorations mentioned in the story.

Prayer

We thank you, dear God, for all the things that make Christmas different and exciting. Help us to enjoy these days at home, at school and at church. Amen

* Mr Bear was greatly surprised when he worked out the problem Timothy had set him. If he'd done his sums correctly, he found that the amount for Christmas Eve alone, by the doubling process, would be £83,886.08. The total from all the 24 windows of your Advent calendar would amount to £166,772.15—a sixth of a million pounds!

See pages 113–115 for decoration templates and instructions.

★

— Day 11 —

Friends!

… in which Miss Read wants a quieter classroom, Lauren shows her artistic talent, and Timothy widens his circle of friends.

Nativity play rehearsals were going really well. Miss Read was delighted with her class for all that they were doing in them. The only trouble was that they were getting noisier in class—all chatter and not enough work.

'If you're not quieter, I'll have to do something about it,' she warned.

There was so much to talk about. Timothy Bear sat next to Claude and they were just as bad as everyone else. Sometimes they would get so carried away that in the middle of class they would hit hand against paw in the air and call out 'Friends'. In the end, Miss Read had had enough and on Monday morning she put her plan into action.

'I'm changing our seating arrangements,' she announced. 'From now on we'll be sitting girl, boy, girl, boy.' The news was greeted with shocked silence.

'That's more like it,' smiled Miss Read. Timothy was now seated next to Lauren instead of Claude, and Claude was over by the window. Lauren! Timothy didn't know much about Lauren except that she was one of the angels in their play and could sing quite well. Timothy turned himself away at a slight angle when Lauren took up her new place. There would be as little contact as possible. Lauren, too, was quite happy about that.

Certainly the whole class was much quieter. Miss Read knew some were upset but she reckoned her plan was working. Timothy complained about the new seating arrangements at home, but Mrs Bear sided with Miss Read.

'Miss Read always has a good reason for what she does,' said Mum. 'The play is doing you a lot of good as well.'

As the school week went by, Timothy did notice one more thing about Lauren. He couldn't help it. Whenever there were spare moments, Lauren would be at work in her small notebook. She was filling it with drawings of other girls in the class, and they were good. Just by glancing, Timothy could tell who Lauren was drawing, and each portrait took a very few moments. Timothy couldn't draw to save his life!

By Friday afternoon, Miss Read knew that the class had had a very good week. The rehearsals were still going splendidly—the one that morning had been brilliant—and in the classroom more work was being done in a quieter atmosphere. Miss Read decided to give over the whole afternoon to picture-making, as a treat. She was keen for her class to think about which way round they should place their pieces of paper. She explained that the different ways could be called 'landscape' and 'portrait'. She suggested that they should draw one of each kind from the Christmas story to establish the names in their minds.

'I find it easier to draw a landscape,' she admitted.

Swiftly she placed a wide piece of paper on her easel and sketched in lines that soon looked like hills around Bethlehem with a stable in the distance.

Then she put a new piece of paper on the easel and turned it round so that it was taller and thinner.

'But I'm hopeless at portraits. I can't draw people very well at all.'

Timothy's paw shot up before he'd had time to think.

'Lauren could draw you a portrait. She's brilliant at them.'

Miss Read smiled. 'What a recommendation, Timothy. Come on, Lauren. You have a go, please, on my board.'

Lauren shyly went to the board with the portrait-shaped paper pinned to it. Miss Read handed Lauren her pens.

'Perhaps you could draw Timothy's portrait for us,' said Miss Read. 'He's a very handsome member of our class.'

Several children giggled but then sat in wonder as, with a few confident lines, Lauren created Timothy's likeness on the paper. After a couple of minutes, it was definitely Timothy staring out at the class.

'That certainly is our innkeeper's boy,' proclaimed Miss Read, leading the class in clapping hands as a thank you.

Lauren returned to her place amid the round of applause. Without thinking, Timothy raised his paws and exchanged 'high fives' with Lauren.

'Friends,' they both said at the same time.

Advent activity

Make a 'landscape' type picture and a 'portrait' type picture.

Prayer

Dear Lord Jesus, help us to be on the look-out for new friends, and teach us to be good friends with those we already have. Amen

— Day 12 —

Sleeping rough

… in which Timothy meets a homeless man, his school plans a special performance of their nativity play, and Timothy gives away his chocolates.

Timothy Bear saw the man stretched out asleep on the bench in the park. Timothy was going there with Mr Bear to practise his football. The man was wearing a woolly red bobble hat.

'Why on earth is he sleeping on a bench?' Timothy wanted to know.

'He could be homeless,' answered Mr Bear. 'Quite a few people are sleeping rough these days.'

Timothy thought of his warm bed. 'I suppose I sleep smooth,' he said quietly.

The man had reminded Timothy of one of the characters in his earliest reading book at school. He wore a red hat, too. 'I shall call him Roger Red Hat,' thought Timothy to himself.

The next time Timothy's class rehearsed the nativity play, Roger Red Hat popped into Timothy's mind. 'Would he even now be sleeping on the bench?' he wondered. But in the play Timothy was going with the innkeeper to the door of the inn. Joseph had knocked on it. It occurred to Timothy that Joseph and Mary were homeless in Bethlehem and about to sleep rough on a stable floor. The shepherds, too, were sleeping rough on the hills around Bethlehem.

There were lots of people like Roger Red Hat in the Christmas story! The wise men and the angels were a long way from their homes. Last of all, there was baby Jesus. Where was his home? And wasn't that feeding trough an uncomfortable place for a baby to sleep? It's a good job that, as the innkeeper's boy, Timothy was keeping an eye on the manger's wobbly leg.

That afternoon, Miss Read needed the help of her class on another matter. Every year they sold tickets for parents and friends to come to the Christmas play and then gave the money away to help others.

'Has anyone any idea about what the money should be used for this year?' Miss Read asked.

Immediately Timothy thought of Roger Red Hat and his paw was up like a rocket.

'Yes, Timothy,' smiled Miss Read.

'There was a lot of homelessness and sleeping rough at Bethlehem for the first Christmas,' started Timothy in what, for him, was a long speech. 'Could we help people who are still homeless round here?'

'What a fantastic idea,' said Miss Read. 'There's a charity just started called "New Hope" that's setting out to help just those people.'

Now several hands were up, and people were making additional suggestions. In the end, as well as the money from tickets going to 'New Hope', it was agreed that Miss Bridge would try to get lists of names so that they could invite homeless people and those sleeping rough to an extra performance of the play and then provide them with a tea afterwards. Timothy remembered the growing collection of chocolates he was saving from his Advent calendar. They would be just right to add to the biscuits and cakes.

The next Saturday, Timothy went with his dad again to the park. He was half hoping to spot Roger Red Hat. Indeed, there he was—not sleeping on the bench this time but sitting on it, eating a bread roll.

'Let's go and meet Roger,' said Timothy to Mr Bear.

'How do you know the man's name?' queried Mr Bear.

'Oh, I don't. That's my pretend name for him.'

The man on the bench was delighted to have company. He was even more delighted when he heard the school's plans for the special performance of their Christmas play—and the tea. He could help pass round invitations to others like him without a home. Mr Bear said he was sure that Miss Bridge would like him to come into school to help with the list.

'I'm sorry,' said Mr Bear, 'but I don't know your name.'

'Roger,' said the man with the woolly red bobble hat. 'Roger Redhead.'

Timothy Bear was not surprised in the least. He'd only got the name a little bit wrong.

Not only did Roger Redhead come in to see Miss Bridge, but Miss Read also heard about him and got him to come and talk to her class about being homeless. The class asked him lots of questions and found out so much.

When it came to the special play performance and tea, Miss Bridge was able to present a cheque for £500 to 'New Hope'. The man in charge of 'New Hope' said that they planned to spend it on special meals for homeless people over Christmas.

Roger Redhead looked across to Timothy. 'It promises to be the best Christmas I've had in years,' said Roger, 'and this chocolate is absolutely delicious.'

Advent activity

Who are the groups of people in our own country who could do with some help? Is there anything you and your family can do to help them?

Prayer

Dear Jesus, you are a friend to those without friends; you help those who are in need; you heal those who are unwell and your life was spent in doing good. Help us to do good, too. Make us strong to do right, gentle with those who are weak, and kind to all who are sad. Amen

The black sheep and the last angel

... in which Miss Read needs one more angel, and May doesn't stand a chance until Timothy's magical encounter with a lonely sheep on the hillside outside Bethlehem.

Miss Read didn't realise it, but May had hoped to be an angel for a long, long time. May knew it was an impossibility, though. Miss Read always chose angels with long blonde hair and blue eyes. May's hair was brown and short, and her eyes were hazel. May was not surprised to hear Miss Read call out her list of angels: girls with fair hair and blue eyes. No mention of May.

'We really need one more,' Miss Read pondered, surveying her class. Timothy Bear was only half attending. He certainly didn't want to be an angel! He was thinking animal thoughts and of all the animals that there might have been at the first Christmas. There must have been sheep around Bethlehem—

the shepherds were looking after them. He was wondering what it was really like in those fields of Bethlehem. He must have wondered very hard. He found himself floating through time and space—spinning but never dizzy, speeding but never frightened—and he landed with the slightest bump.

Timothy Bear shivered. It was much colder than in his school. It was dark, too. A wood fire glowed, a stone's throw away. Shepherds and sheep were settling down to make themselves comfortable for the long night.

One lamb, next to Timothy, was apart from the flock. She bleated a whispered welcome: 'It's good of you to come. It's nice to have company for a change.' The lamb went on to explain, 'The others leave me out; I'm different from them. They say that when I grow up I'll be a black sheep.'

'You look all white to me,' whispered Timothy in the dark.

'It doesn't show much at night,' the lamb said quietly, 'but I'm really quite grey... What on earth?!'

A bright light had appeared in the night sky. It came nearer and nearer in the growing shape of a person. The gaze of shepherds and sheep, and bear, were drawn to it, riveted.

Then a voice sang out clearly, 'Don't be afraid! I have good news for you, which will make everyone happy. This very day in King David's home town a Saviour was born for you. He is Christ the Lord. You will know who he is, because you will find him dressed in baby clothes and lying on a bed of hay.'

The voice stopped but then the whole sky was alight. An angel choir was singing, 'Praise God in heaven! Peace on earth to everyone who pleases God.'

The light faded as quickly as it had started. Shepherds and

sheep, and bear, held their breath, trying to take it all in.

'Come with me,' said the lamb to Timothy. 'Let's go to Bethlehem.'

Timothy needed no second bidding. Lamb and bear scurried across the fields, racing each other, company for each other. Timothy looked back at the shepherds, who were sorting out who should stay watching the flocks and who should go down to Bethlehem. As it happened, the longer legs of the shepherds made up the ground and they all arrived at the stable together. It was just as the angel had said it would be: a man and a woman inside, gazing in wonder at the manger containing the newborn baby.

The shepherds stopped in the low doorway, awestruck. Timothy hugged the shadows but the lamb crept fearlessly up to the feeding trough. Gently her forelegs eased up on to the rim of the manger, her eyes taking in the sight of the baby so close. Baby and lamb seemed to exchange glances of love and understanding. The lamb felt she really belonged at last.

Timothy knew that his time in Bethlehem was done. A shepherd came forward to pick up the lamb with tenderness and care. Timothy was once again floating through time and space—spinning but never dizzy, speeding but never frightened—and he landed with the slightest bump.

Miss Read was still wondering about the final angel. Timothy saw May's sad, wistful face and somehow now understood.

'Perhaps May could be the final angel?' said Timothy Bear

quietly. The class smiled at the way Timothy had asked. Miss Read smiled, too. 'I don't see why not. Would you like to be an angel, May?'

May didn't have to say anything. Her delight was written all over her face. As the rehearsals went by, Miss Read noticed it was May's singing in the angelic choir that kept all the other angels together and in tune.

In the end, Timothy heard his teacher say to May, 'May, you really are an angel,' and Timothy couldn't help thinking as well of a lamb who felt she belonged for the first time at the first Christmas.

Advent activity

Make a cardboard sheep and, if you get permission, hang it up on a Christmas tree or as another Christmas decoration.

Prayer

Give us courage, Lord Jesus, if we ever feel left out, and give us courage not to allow anyone we know to be left out. Amen

★

— Day 14 —

Grandma's brooch

… in which Claude sets up a wise men's gang, Timothy remembers what helped him to be a good wise man, and with Grandma's permission Timothy sets Claude on the same path.

Timothy Bear had to get used to the idea of his best friend, Claude, being the wise man who would give baby Jesus gold in the school nativity play. Timothy would have liked Miss Read to have chosen him for that part. He had been that wise man at church last year. Even though he was disappointed, Timothy still agreed that his cloak and his crown from a year earlier could be altered to fit Claude. Claude's mum couldn't possibly make a costume, so again Miss Read was grateful for Timothy's help.

Claude didn't seem so grateful. He thought being a wise man gave him the right to be bossy. He said to Timothy, 'Make sure my cloak is always hung up properly on its hanger.' Then again, 'Make sure my crown is stored on the top shelf. I don't want it squashed.'

Miss Read had put Timothy in charge of keeping things tidy and in their right place, but Claude could have done some of his own tidying-up. One or two pleases wouldn't have come amiss—and whose cloak and crown were they, anyway?

Claude was the same on the playground. David was chosen to be the wise man to bring frankincense, and Michael brought the myrrh. Claude said they should be the wise men's gang. They went round giving their orders and throwing their weight about. They had no time and no room in their gang for shepherds and certainly not for an innkeeper's boy. Timothy missed having Claude as a friend.

When it came to the rehearsals, Miss Read noticed that the wise men were getting careless about their part in the play. She had said right from the beginning, 'Slowly, wise men. Heads up straight. Carry your gifts carefully.'

Gradually the wise men were becoming sloppy. They were being silly walking up to the manger from the back of the hall and travelling much too quickly.

'Claude,' she pointed out, 'you should be setting the example. You lead the others with the gold.'

But Claude sauntered up, round-shouldered, with his cloak slipping off and his crown on crooked. Miss Read was cross when she spotted that Claude was even carrying his gift behind his back. 'Claude!' she stormed. 'Slowly. Head up straight. Carefully.'

Timothy Bear remembered when he was the wise man who carried gold in church. He remembered what had helped him so much. Grandma had loaned him her lion's-head brooch to pin his cloak high up round his neck. It was brilliant. Not only did it look good but it kept his cloak in place and it made him hold his head up straight.

'It will make you as good as gold,' his grandma had said. Timothy smiled. It had worked for him. That very evening, when they visited Grandma, Timothy asked if Claude could borrow the lion's head.

'Certainly,' said Grandma. 'Does he need to be as good as gold?' she asked, smiling. Timothy smiled back. If only Grandma knew.

Early next day, Timothy found Claude in the playground. The other wise men were not around. Claude was amazed that Timothy had arranged the loan of such a special item for him.

'Grandma says it makes the wearer as good as gold,' said Timothy. Claude was shamefaced. He had let the wise man business go to his head. He realised that wise men don't have to be bossy and bigheaded.

'Thank you, Timothy,' said Claude softly. 'It's just what I need.'

Miss Read was thrilled with the wise men's contribution to that day's rehearsal. Claude set a magnificent example. He led the wise men so slowly, head held so straight, holding the gold so carefully in front of him, crown on his head so regally. David and Michael followed Claude's example. Claude then spoke his words slowly, loudly and clearly.

'Gold I bring because Jesus is king.'

'Well done, all of you,' said Miss Read as the whole cast held its finishing position, having sung 'Come and join the celebration'.

'You wise men were especially magnificent. Claude, I think it must have something to do with that lion's-head brooch you have at your neck. You were as good as gold.'

Claude smiled a great big smile. It was smiled mostly in the direction of Timothy Bear.

Advent activity

Make a picture or a cut-out of a lion's head. You may be able to find out about a lion called Aslan in some famous stories.

Prayer

Dear Lord Jesus, help us to learn to cope with times when we feel bossed about, and save us from being bossy ourselves. Amen

★

— Day 15 —

Giving presents

... in which Timothy thinks about giving presents, not only getting them, he and David make a magical journey together to find out about frankincense, and in the end Timothy has his present ready for his grandpa.

For the first time in his life, Timothy Bear was thinking about the presents he would give for Christmas this year as well as the presents he hoped to get. It was his present to Grandpa that had sparked it all off. On a family walk in the woods, shuffling through the fallen leaves looking for conkers, Timothy had spotted a length of wood with a bulge at one end. He'd picked it up and, in a moment of brainwave, realised it might be perfect for his grandpa as a walking stick. Mr Bear tried it out and confirmed that it was just the right length.

'The only trouble is, it hasn't cost me anything,' said Timothy.

'It's the thought that counts,' responded Mrs Bear. 'You could always wrap some of your pictures with it.'

Timothy saw the sense of that.

At school, David had a problem about his part in the nativity play. David had been chosen as the wise man who brings frankincense to baby Jesus. It was when Timothy and David were tidying up the stage in the hall that David mentioned what was troubling him.

'But I don't know what frankincense is,' said David to Timothy. 'At first, I thought I was bringing Frankenstein.'

Timothy smiled. He had thought exactly the same.

'Sometimes,' whispered Timothy, 'if I wonder about something really hard, I get to find out what it was really like. But I've never done it with anyone else before.'

'Let's see,' said David just as quietly. 'Let's sit on this stage block and wonder.' They did just that. They must have both wondered equally hard, for they found themselves floating through time and space—spinning but never dizzy, speeding but never frightened. They landed with the slightest bump, still together.

They were in some kind of camp and all was activity around them. The sun was setting over the desert. A young man was carefully placing a silver container in the side carrier bag of a well-behaved camel. The young man was not in the least surprised to be in the company of Timothy and David.

'Hello, you two,' he began. 'Seeing us off on our journey? That's good of you. The star should appear very soon.'

David, too, was taking everything in his stride.

'Please, what is it that you're storing so carefully in the camel's luggage?'

'That silver container holds the finest juice or sap from

some trees of our country. It's called frankincense and when the top of the flask is removed the smell is fantastic.'

'Where are you taking it?' asked Timothy, half knowing what the answer would be.

'We're on a journey following a star to find a brand new king who has been born for everyone in the world. This king has come from God so I'm bringing my best gift to say thank you.'

'You're being very careful. It's taking you a long time,' pointed out David.

'We have a saying in our country,' smiled the young man. 'An important part of a present is in the journey to get it to the right person.'

Timothy Bear remembered his walk in the woods.

'We have a saying like that,' said Timothy. 'It's the thought that counts.'

'Isn't it a small world?' grinned the young man. 'Look—there's our star.'

Indeed, it was now dark enough and the star could be seen above where the sun had set. David and Timothy stared at the star in wonder. But their time in the desert was done. They were once again floating through time and space—spinning but never dizzy, speeding but never frightened—and they landed back on the stage block with the slightest bump, still together.

David went to the back of the hall to make sure his silver container was safe. It was a shame that it only pretended to contain that wonderful sap with the fantastic scent.

Later that evening, Timothy gathered together all his

picture-making pencils and paints. He would make such pictures for his grandpa—pictures of the times they shared together. His favourite picture would be of grandpa and grandcub striding through the woods, Grandpa swinging a walking stick with a bulge at one end.

Advent activity

Timothy made his own present for Grandpa. Think of some people, not too many, for whom you might make a special present this Christmas.

Prayer

Dear God, help us to be as good at giving as we are at getting. Amen

— Day 16 —

Goldie

… in which events make Michael, the bringer of myrrh, very sad, but he bravely goes ahead with the dress rehearsal and finds himself comforted.

Timothy Bear had really wanted to be a wise man in the nativity play, but not really the wise man who presented Jesus with myrrh. Somehow, myrrh sounded a sad thing to be bringing. Anyway, it was Michael whom Miss Read asked to be that wise man. She chose Michael because he was a serious-looking boy whose face rarely lit up with smiles.

Miss Read explained what myrrh is. 'It's rather like frankincense,' she told her class. 'It's the gum or sap taken from a tree. It is used especially in hot countries to anoint the bodies of people who have died.'

Michael thought it was cool to be presenting myrrh. 'But why give it to a baby who has just been born?' he wanted to know.

'Well,' said Miss Read, 'I think it was because Jesus would

die when he was a young man, and the way that he died is still remembered all over the world.'

Nearer and nearer came the time for the public performances of this year's Christmas play. At last they were to have the dress rehearsal, when, as well as costumes being complete, Linda would be operating the lights with different coloured effects. Miss Read said they would have their dress rehearsal as late as they could in afternoon school.

'Then you'll get used to it being almost as dark as when your parents come,' she told them.

The evening before the dress rehearsal, tragedy struck Michael and his family. No one knew who had left the front gate open. Their dog, Goldie, was quite old; he was not quick enough dashing across the road, and the advancing car had no chance of avoiding him in the gathering gloom. Goldie was killed instantly. Michael and his family buried Goldie that very evening in their back garden.

'It's not fair,' groaned Michael. 'It's going to spoil Christmas. Bad things shouldn't happen near Christmas.'

Michael's dad wasn't so sure about that. He remembered what King Herod had done, the first Christmas. He told Michael that King Herod had had baby boys in Bethlehem killed by his soldiers but Jesus had just escaped. Michael didn't feel any better.

The next morning, Michael wasn't sure that he felt like going ahead with the nativity play rehearsal. His mum said he should give school a try. Michael looked even more serious than usual when he did get to school. He could only just manage to tell his friends what had happened to Goldie without crying. Michael's mum had let Miss Read know about it.

'Michael is going to do his best,' Miss Read told the class. 'Michael, you might find it helpful in the end.'

The dress rehearsal went reasonably well. There were one or two things that Miss Read reckoned would come 'right on the night' of their first performance. The three wise men made their way forward from the back of the hall—slowly, heads up straight—carefully carrying their gifts. Michael's face was not only serious but sad as well. Today, he didn't have to act the part for carrying myrrh.

Linda gradually increased the lighting in the hall as the three wise men neared the stable. Light reflected back off the silver star hanging above the stable's roof. The wise men arrived and knelt at the manger. That was the moment for Linda to turn on the switch that directed a golden beam of light right into the manger. The whole cast gasped in wonder at the golden glow that embraced baby Jesus' cradle.

'Goldie,' thought Michael to himself. Then it was his turn to speak as he presented his gift of myrrh. He spoke in his clearest voice: 'I bring myrrh for the king born to die, for the king that comforts us now.'

In that moment, Michael felt a special comfort just for him.

Advent activity

Make a list of anyone you know, people near to you or people you've heard about in the world, who are sad at the present time.

Prayer

Take the list you have made in your Advent activity and pray for the people on it.

Timothy Bear and the Christmas card

… in which Timothy's family receive Christmas cards and are busy, and Timothy has a fantastic meeting with a small camel and a small baby before returning to his busy family.

It was getting nearer and nearer to Christmas. It really was. Christmas cards were arriving by almost every post. Timothy and Teresa would hold the cards and pass them to Mum, who stood on some steps and pegged the cards to strings hanging from the picture rail.

One evening, Timothy was trying to spot as many animals as he could on the hanging cards. Mr and Mrs Bear still had some rushing about to do. Auntie Gladys, who always stayed for Christmas, was dozing in her chair. Teresa was having a temper tantrum and had stormed upstairs. Sisters!

One card in the row hanging above the television set caught Timothy's eye. It was a picture of the three wise men riding through hill country on camels. A star shone in the sky ahead. One camel, smaller than the rest, had no rider—only bags containing luggage at her sides.

Timothy stared at the picture, wondering hard. He could almost hear the bells that were hanging round the camels' necks. He must have wondered very hard indeed, because suddenly he seemed to be floating through time and space—spinning but never dizzy, speeding but never frightened.

He landed with the slightest bump, swaying from side to side—and he really could hear the camel bells!

Timothy was holding on to a hairy neck, the neck of the smallest camel on the card, and they were moving. The wise men wrapped their bright robes around them as the sky darkened towards night. A fresh breeze ruffled Timothy Bear's fur.

'Nice of you to drop on,' said a voice. 'What's your name?'

'Timothy, thank you. What's yours?'

'Clara,' said the camel, 'and it's nearly my bedtime.'

'They look very important,' said Timothy, pointing to the wise men.

'Well, they are,' replied Clara. 'They boss me about. Many's the whipping I've had from them. They've got a lot on their minds—kingdoms to run, budgets to work out, reputations to look after. But they seem to be changing. They suddenly decided to leave their kingdoms behind them. They've never torn themselves away before. Things are looking up; they've been looking up—looking up to that star.

'Perhaps that's the difference. They've always looked down before, to count money or eat their feasts or check their lists.

But since they started to see that star, it's been much easier to get on with them. Why, they're almost human. The other day, they even lightened my loads.'

'Hey! That's sudden!' cried Timothy Bear.

Clara had skidded to a halt along with the others, and Timothy grabbed pawfuls of hair.

'Are we there? It's only an ordinary house.'

Timothy stayed where he was as the wise men dismounted. One wise man went to the door and turned to the others, nodding and smiling.

'I haven't seen him smile like that in all my life,' whispered Clara.

The wise men went inside. Timothy could hear happy chatter and, from time to time, a baby gurgling. Then the first wise man came out and made straight for Clara. He led her right inside the house. Timothy clung on, stroking her neck.

'The baby camel and the baby boy,' announced a voice.

'And the baby bear,' thought Timothy.

The wise men undid the bags at Clara's side and out came presents. They were strange, expensive presents. Timothy wished he had a ball or a car that he could give. The wise men were bowing, and Clara again whispered her surprise into Timothy's ear. 'All the time, people bow to them. He's a very special baby. He's making all the difference to them and to me.'

'And to me,' whispered back Timothy.

That was the last he said to Clara. Again he was floating through time and space—spinning but never dizzy, speeding but never frightened. With the slightest bump he was back with his drawings and the card was in its place above the television. Mrs Bear rushed in to check the time.

'Look at this card,' said Timothy. 'It's special.'

'Me! Look at a card, with cakes in the oven? Christmas is just around the corner, you know!'

Auntie Gladys stirred in her chair.

'Please, Auntie, look over here.'

'Yes, my dear… but… I'm so sleepy…' and Auntie Gladys nodded off to sleep again.

Mr Bear came in to look in the sideboard.

'Please look at this card with me.'

'Sorry, not now. The bulb needs replacing in the cupboard under the stairs.'

Teresa was Timothy's last hope, but when he called upstairs she told him in no uncertain terms that she was getting her doll dressed for a party. Timothy sighed. His family were just as bad as those wise men before they looked up. Perhaps they would look up soon. He had, and he would never forget it.

Something fell from his paw on to the carpet. He smiled as he picked it up. It was a tuft of camel's hair.

Advent activity

Make your own Christmas card about one part of the Christmas story, and decide who you will send it to.

Prayer

We thank you for the wise men, dear God, who made their long journey to Bethlehem, and for the star that guided them. We thank you for all the ways you are guiding us to Christmas this year. Amen

— Day 18 —

Auntie's mince pies

… in which Timothy's class goes carol singing but his rumbling tummy threatens to spoil the sweet sounds of the choir, until Auntie Dorothy's generous gift saves the day.

One of the best things about the nativity play was the quality and the volume of the singing. Those not fortunate enough to get an acting part were really throwing themselves heart and soul—and voice—into the Christmas songs and carols. Miss Read thought it was so good that she arranged to take her class on a visit to their local residential care home to sing the songs from the nativity play.

'I'll let your parents know,' announced Miss Read, 'and we'll go at the end of school, just as it's getting dark. It will be real carol singing.'

The class buzzed with excitement at the prospect. Timothy Bear was particularly excited as he realised that his Auntie Dorothy was one of the residents at the home. Mrs Bear made sure Auntie Dorothy knew about the coming visit so that she could get excited too.

When the afternoon came, it was one of the coldest days they had had that winter. Scarves and gloves were the order of the day. Timothy was grateful as well that his fur kept him so warm, but he was feeling very hungry inside. Timothy's resolution to give up honey and sweets before Christmas was really working, but it did make him feel hungry between meals.

Miss Read gathered her class together outside the care home. They would sing a couple of songs there in the cold before giving their concert inside.

'We'll start with a quiet one,' suggested Miss Read. '"Born in the night, Mary's child". One, two, three, four!' The class sang the song unaccompanied so very well. Timothy Bear knows that he's a bit of a growler when it comes to singing. Miss Read had even suggested in the play that he could just whisper the words of the songs! But in this quiet carol it was Timothy's hungry rumbling tummy that began to be heard. Outside in the open air, people didn't notice too much. Then Miss Read suggested they should sing 'We wish you a merry Christmas'. When they got to the verse about wanting figgy pudding, that made Timothy feel even hungrier (not that he was sure what figgy pudding would taste like).

Moments later, the class were in the spacious lounge, getting into their places. Timothy looked round at the smiling elderly faces. No Auntie Dorothy. He whispered to the kind lady who had let them in and seemed to be in charge.

'I was expecting to see my Auntie Dorothy.'

'Let's ask your teacher if we can go up to her room and

see what's happened,' replied the kind lady.

They rang the bell to Auntie's room. In the end, Auntie Dorothy opened the door, blinking in surprise.

'Oh dear,' she said. 'I've been asleep. Have I missed your concert?' Timothy shook his head.

'Wait a minute and I'll be ready.'

A minute later, Auntie Dorothy was back with a big round cake tin that she handed to the lady in charge.

'Here's what I promised,' said Auntie.

The carol concert was a great success. The class sang out and their smiling faces matched the faces of their audience. Most of the carols were songs that needed full volume and the loudest voices. Timothy's rumbling tum was not noticed, but he knew that they were finishing with 'Away in a manger' and that Miss Read wanted it sung quietly and sweetly.

Before they reached the last carol, however, the kind lady in charge stood up and said how pleased everyone was that the class had come on their visit.

'As a treat,' she went on, 'Dorothy has made us some mince pies to enjoy before you bring our concert to a close. And, children, don't worry about the crumbs. My dog makes a wonderful hoover!'

Timothy Bear couldn't remember having a mince pie before, but his Auntie Dorothy had made them so they were sure to be good. They were! Timothy's mince pie was delicious and it filled the space in his tummy perfectly. Timothy remembered to whisper his way through 'Away in a manger'. His voice did not spoil the sweetness of the singing... and neither did his tummy.

Advent activity

Make a list of the Christmas songs you would sing if you, like Timothy, visited a residential care home for elderly people. How many of the words can you remember?

Prayer

Lord Jesus, we pray for all people who do not live in their own homes. Cheer them this Christmas as they remember that you were born in a borrowed stable. Amen

— Day 19 —

The candy cane

... in which Timothy hears a talk at church about a special sweet that helps him understand who Jesus is. The very next day, Timothy passes on the message. Perhaps Miss Read will buy her class one of the sweets each for Christmas.

The part of the innkeeper's boy in the nativity play was a speaking part. It must have been the shortest speech on record but it was vital to the play. It came very near the end. The whole cast was assembled round the manger in Bethlehem's stable—the shepherds, the angels, the wise men, Mary and Joseph—everyone. At that moment, Timothy Bear was to step forward right next to the manger and ask loudly, slowly and clearly, 'Who is he?' Joseph would give the answer, 'He is Jesus—God's Son, our Saviour.' That was the signal for everyone to sing 'Come and join the celebration'.

It was strange that, the Sunday before the performances, the speaker in church asked the same question about Jesus: 'Who is he?' He said that as Christmas was such a busy time, with so much to remember, he would tell the story of a special sweet that was made to remind people about who Jesus is. Best of all, he had one of the sweets for each member of the congregation to take home with them. It would jog their memories.

The speaker began his story. 'Our sweetmaker lived in America, and in America some sweets are called candy. He made a special candy cane to celebrate Jesus' birth.'

Even though Timothy had given up sweets in the run-up to Christmas, he was fascinated by what the speaker had to say. The candy cane did indeed do its job of keeping the talk clear in Timothy's mind. He took it with him to school the next day, hoping that Miss Read would let him take part in that afternoon's 'Show and Tell' time. It worked out perfectly. For once, no other paw or hand was up in the air, only Timothy's.

'Well, the floor is yours,' smiled Miss Read, 'and there's still ten minutes of school to go.'

'Who is he?' began Timothy Bear theatrically. Many were now smiling. One or two giggled. 'This might help us remember who Jesus is,' went on Timothy, and he produced the candy cane. Timothy remembered the way the speaker of the day before had delivered his talk by asking questions. He decided on the same approach. 'What is the main colour of the candy?' Timothy pointed to Laura.

'White,' she said quietly.

'Yes, white, because Jesus is pure and good,' said Timothy. 'And what letter does this look like?' Timothy held the cane so that the curved bit was hanging down.

'J for Jesus,' said Claude.

Timothy turned the cane up the other way. 'What does it look like now?'

'My grandad's walking stick,' said Amanda.

'Not bad,' admitted Timothy, but Sanjay, one of the shepherds, had his hand up.

'It's the shape of one of our crooks that we use to keep the sheep in their place.'

Timothy nodded. It was all going rather well! 'But what about the red stripe?'

This time it was Michael, the wise man who brings myrrh, wanting to answer. 'Does the red stripe remind us that Jesus' death was going to be so important?' Again Timothy was nodding.

'There's one other thing I can remember,' went on Timothy. 'The candymaker added peppermint to remind us of the spices the wise men brought to Jesus.

'That's it,' finished Timothy. He had run out of things to say.

'Let's give our innkeeper's boy a clap,' said a delighted Miss Read. 'What a shame we haven't all got a candy cane to take home with us, but I have seen them in the shops, and I do like to give you a little something for Christmas. It would celebrate so much about our nativity play—it would be a sweet reminder.'

This time the class decided to give Miss Read a clap. It might encourage her to visit the shops.

Advent activity

Try to find a shop that sells candy canes and, if you are allowed to buy one, try to remember what the different colours and shapes tell you about Jesus.

Prayer

Dear Lord Jesus, we thank you that Christmas celebrates your birthday, and we ask that we will go on finding out more and more about you. Amen

— Day 20 —

Party time!

… in which Timothy Bear wonders about the animals there must have been in Bethlehem; he wonders so hard that he is taken on a journey to find out, it's a grumpy stable to begin with but in the end they all have a party, and possibly the angels have a party too.

To Timothy Bear's mind, there weren't nearly enough animals in Miss Read's nativity play. In fact, there was only one— the donkey that carried Mary all the way from Nazareth to Bethlehem.

Matthew had been given the part of the donkey. He was draped in a brown cloth, and two cricket stumps in his hands played the part of his two front legs. Only Matthew's mum in the audience would know that the donkey was indeed Matthew. But Timothy thought there must have been several animals around baby Jesus. After all, he was put in a manger and a manger must have once held food for animals. And shepherds look after sheep!

'I suppose the wise men must have come by camel,' said Timothy to himself. 'But, other than the smallest camel, they were too big to enter a stable.'

Timothy wondered how the animals would have celebrated the birth of the baby in their stable. Animals love a party! Timothy must have wondered very hard. He found himself floating through time and space—spinning but never dizzy, speeding but never frightened—and he landed with the slightest bump.

It was very dark. There were strong smells. His ears were hearing confused animal conversations. Slowly his eyes grew used to his surroundings. A little starlight came through gaps in the roof. The other animals were not in the least surprised that Timothy had joined them, but there was nothing like a party going on. In fact, a cow was having her bad-tempered say.

'What a lot of fuss!' she moaned, mooing moodily. 'We can hardly move and now we've been invaded by humans. It was bad enough when there were just two of them but our feeding trough has been taken over by their human calf.'

Timothy Bear was sure he knew where he was, but he was still surprised when he heard himself speaking out.

'Steady on. Don't you realise who that baby is? It's baby Jesus, born to be king.'

'Stuff and nonsense!' retorted the grumpy cow. 'A king born here?' She lowed a laugh, hard and bitter.

A donkey took over from the cow and Timothy was glad to hear that he spoke more gently.

'A king, you say? I've carried his mum a long way and she

didn't seem like a princess. And kings can cause wars and fighting.'

'This king is different,' said Timothy, feeling a bit better. 'He's a king of love and peace. In fact, when he grows up he will ride into a city on a donkey to show that he comes in gentleness and not with an army of soldiers.'

'We could do with a king like that,' brayed the donkey. 'I'm going to have a closer look while they're all asleep.'

There was a sad bleat at Timothy's side.

'I'm too small for anyone to ride,' sobbed a sheep. 'I'm not much use at all.'

'Don't think like that,' said Timothy. 'When that baby grows up, he's going to tell a story about a lost sheep. The lost sheep gets found by a good shepherd. That one sheep is so special that they have a party to celebrate.'

The sad sheep had cheered up. The worried donkey came back enchanted. Even the grumpy cow had been listening carefully and was brightening up.

'Perhaps we should have a party,' she said, 'to celebrate a new life.'

'Yes,' joined in the donkey. 'I'm all for a bit of a knees-up.'

'I'll do a charade of a nursery rhyme,' said the sheep, who now felt quite special herself. She pretended to stagger across the stable with heavy loads on her back. Then she came back and did it again.

'I know,' said a calf that Timothy now noticed for the first time, 'Baa, baa, black sheep.'

The sheep nodded and smiled with pleasure. Timothy took off his scarf and they played Blind Animal's Bluff. Then it was a game of Sleeping Lions. They didn't want to wake the baby by making too much noise.

It seemed to Timothy that it was a good time to leave, while the stable party was in full swing. He was once again floating through time and space. As he left the stable, high in the sky he caught a glimpse of a cloud of angels—and they seemed to turn for a moment, kicking their feet in the air. Perhaps they were having a knees-up, too!

Timothy was spinning but never dizzy, speeding but never frightened, and he landed with the slightest bump. There had been an animals' party to celebrate the first Christmas, after all.

Advent activity

Make a list of party games you enjoy. You might be able to think of more games to do with the world of animals.

Prayer

Dear Lord Jesus, we thank you that animals had their part to play in the Christmas story and that your coming makes a difference to the whole of creation. Amen

— Day 21 —

The performance

... in which it's time at last to perform the nativity play, but the audience arrives noisily. Timothy puts up a notice with one or two spelling mistakes, and the audience appreciate an excellent performance.

It was the evening of the main performance of the nativity play. It had been on everyone's mind all day. Every preparation had been made that could be made, but now the class was coping with its nervousness. Even Miss Read was nervous!

'It's all part of giving our best,' said Miss Read to her tense and excited class. 'Being nervous shows that it all means a lot to us.'

Timothy Bear's first task when he came back to school was to check that everything was in order in the hall and all the props were in their right place. What he hadn't expected was that the audience was already arriving—adults, parents, brothers, sisters and friends.

How noisy they all were! Miss Bridge would never allow

her school to assemble chatting and knocking into chairs. Some of the grown-ups were even speaking on their mobile phones. Such a restless audience would spoil the play. Timothy must do something! Miss Read was much too busy back in the classroom, getting everyone ready.

There was a spare movable display board by the door, just right for a notice that Timothy could make. He knew where there were some felt-tipped pens and a large piece of cardboard. On the notice, he would ask the audience to please keep their noise down and to please switch off their mobiles.

His spelling was perfect until he left the 'i' out of 'noise' and then put an extra 'o' in 'mobiles'. 'Please keep your nose down and switch off your moobiles,' the notice said. Perhaps he had cows on his mind!

Some in the audience saw Timothy pin up his notice. Some nudged each other and smiled. Others tapped their noses and grinned. The audience was delighted; they became much quieter. Not a single mobile was left on. Everyone prepared themselves to enjoy the play.

What a play it turned out to be! Amanda set the standard with her performance as Mary. Her conversation with the angel was clear and dramatic. Joseph was so attentive and, when he brought on the donkey, the donkey almost skipped in a most amusing and undonkey-like way. The singing of 'Little donkey' set the standard for all the other songs. The audience heard every word. The innkeeper was stressed and short-tempered when Joseph knocked at his door. Timothy Bear, as the innkeeper's boy, led the couple and their donkey much more gently to the stable. 'Born in the night' was sung softly but so very sweetly.

The shepherds had their crooks and their slings with the pompom stones. They acted the part of defending their sheep from the wild animals with great energy and then stood stock-still at the approach of the angels. The angels glided and shimmered in contrast to the rough-and-ready shepherds. They delivered their vital message about a special birth in Bethlehem in a stable. Moments later, the shepherds were arriving at the stable and finding it all just as the angels had told them. Then it was the turn of the wise men, led by Claude, setting a fine example bringing gold.

'Linda the lights' operated her switches without a single mistake and the darkness of the night did much to enhance her work. The whole cast assembled and Timothy asked his question, 'Who is he?' The answer came, that he was Jesus—God's Son, our Saviour.

The whole school launched into 'Come and join the celebration' with tuneful gusto. What a celebration, indeed! Even the audience joined in the chorus with increasing enthusiasm.

> *Come and join the celebration.*
> *There's a new king born today!*

The applause echoed round the hall, loud and long. Some members of the audience even stood up, making it a standing ovation. A few brushed away tears of pride and happiness. At last, Miss Bridge judged it the right moment to move forward to conclude the evening with her thanks. She was pink with pride and she had a special word for the audience.

'In all my years of being here for public performances,' she pointed out, 'I have never known a better audience. You even lifted the performance. It's a wonderful example of adults and children working together.'

A mum in the front row joined in. She turned the display panel round so that Miss Bridge and the school could see Timothy's notice.

'I think this had something to do with it,' said the smiling mum.

Miss Bridge smiled, too. 'I think I recognise the hand-writing,' she said, and then paused. 'Or should I say, the paw-writing. I see we still have some work to do in improving our spelling.'

To everyone's enjoyment, Timothy tried to hide himself behind his paws and the audience broke into even more applause.

Advent activity

Talk about times when adults and children do good things together with each other. How can adults help children and how can children help adults?

Prayer

Dear Lord Jesus, we thank you when things come together so well, like a play performed. We thank you for the time when everything came perfectly together for you to be born, at the first Christmas. Amen

★

— Day 22 —

Josephus Bear

... in which the class has an end-of-term concert, Timothy brings in Mrs Bear's story to be read and then sings a solo to celebrate himself, Josephus Bear and all other cuddly toys.

Miss Read was thrilled with her class. The nativity play had been wonderfully performed. Now it was the end of term.

'On the last afternoon,' Miss Read told her class, 'we'll have a concert among ourselves. You might say a poem, tell a joke, sing a song or something else. I'll make a list of what you want to do.'

There were lots of volunteers. It would make a great end to the term. Last of all, Miss Read noticed Timothy Bear's paw up in the air. She nodded.

'I'll sing a carol that has a line about me in it!'

There were lots of smiles and Miss Read did wonder if it would be safe to let Timothy sing a solo. He's known to be a bit of a growler!

'What's it all about, Timothy?' wondered Miss Read.

'It's a long story,' replied Timothy, very seriously. 'I'll get my mum to write it all down. Perhaps, Miss Read, you'll read what she writes and then I'll sing the song?'

Miss Read agreed. She was half expecting not to hear any more about it, but next morning Timothy arrived at school with an envelope. When Miss Read read what was inside, she thought it would be quite safe to go ahead with the story and the song. In fact, she left it until the last item in the concert. So, just before the end of school, Miss Read began to read aloud what Mrs Bear had written down.

'For some time Timothy has been anxious that the animals in Bethlehem should be more recognised for the part they played when Jesus was born. He even reckons there should be a bear in the story. Here's the story I've made up for him.'

Miss Read paused and looked round at all the upturned faces of her class. You could have heard a pin drop. Miss Read went on reading what Mrs Bear had written.

'A long time ago in Bethlehem there lived a toymaker. He was a very good craftsman and children liked his toys. He made rag balls, wooden soldiers and things like that. He made animal shapes out of materials and stuffed them with wood shavings and sheep's wool. One day he tried to make a bear, but it looked so real that children were frightened and didn't want it. So the toymaker threw the bear down in the corner of his workroom, where it lay forgotten. Some wood shavings escaped through a hole in its paw.

'Later, the toymaker was doing so well that he was offered an important job in the toy department of a large Jerusalem shop. He moved away, and it so happened that he rented his house to Mary, Joseph and the growing baby Jesus. They couldn't live in the stable for ever. They were grateful to have more room, anyway, and fewer draughts.

'Of course, Jesus cried a lot when his teeth started pushing through his tiny gums. Mary wondered how she could help him. One day, she spotted the forgotten bear lying in the corner and pointed him out to Joseph. "He looks a bit fierce," said Joseph. "Let me give him a kinder face, and I'll put a stitch or two in that paw."

'Mary and Joseph were delighted when Jesus held the bear and gurgled with pleasure. "We will call him Josephus Bear," announced Mary, and Joseph was as pleased as punch.

'After a little while, an angel came to Joseph to say that the family must move to Egypt. Wicked King Herod was planning horrible things. So Mary and Joseph prepared for another journey, and I hope you can guess what was the first thing that they gave to Jesus to comfort him.'

Miss Read had finished what Mrs Bear had written and she paused. Many of the class softly whispered, 'Josephus Bear.' Miss Read nodded. 'And now Timothy has his carol for us. He tells me it goes to the tune of "Away in a manger".'

For the first time in his life, Timothy Bear stood up to sing to an audience, and this is what he sang:

When the baby grew older
And his first teeth came through,
Then little Lord Jesus had some crying to do.
And only Josephus could comfort him there,
So they cuddled each other, the baby and bear.

That's why all the children
Should have a bear too,
So when they need comfort, they'll know what to do.
His name will not matter, he has much love to share;
It might be Josephus or Timothy Bear.

The class burst out clapping. The concert had come to a good conclusion. It was time to go home and Christmas was just around the corner.

Advent activity

Draw a picture portrait gallery of your favourite cuddly toys or your favourite story characters.

Prayer

Lord God, thank you for all the ways you give us to find comfort. Thank you for all our toys that give us so much enjoyment. Amen

— Day 23 —

The Christingle tree

... in which the Bear family decorate a tree for the Christmas tree festival, it becomes the centrepiece of the Christingle service, and Timothy discovers he can take the light of Jesus to a dark world.

Timothy's church were organising a Christmas tree festival. Families in the church had volunteered to decorate a Christmas tree each, around a Christmas theme. There were to be 18 trees in total and the Bear family had said they would be responsible for one of them.

The local garden nursery would supply the trees. One of the dads, who was so good at electrical work that he had the nickname Sparks, would arrange for each tree to have its own set of lights. The festival would make a wonderful backdrop for this year's Christingle service, which was always held on an evening two or three days before Christmas.

'This year it's on the eve of Christmas Eve,' said Timothy, pleased with his own cleverness.

Mrs Bear found out that the theme for their tree was to

be 'Christingle'. When she passed on the news, her family greeted it in silence. They had guessed they might get 'shepherds' or 'the three wise men'. Timothy had hoped they might get 'the stable' so that he could make lots of animal pictures to hang from the branches. He'd even forgotten what a Christingle was.

'Well,' said Mum, 'the basic part of a Christingle is an orange.'

'Great,' said Timothy. 'How are we supposed to make a Christmas tree look like an orange?'

'Don't worry,' replied Mum. 'The orange in a Christingle is a picture of our world, and a Christmas tree can stand for our green world just as well.'

She went on to explain that a Christingle orange has a red ribbon round it to show that Jesus died for the whole world—things and animals as well as people.

'We'll put rows and rows of red beads round the middle of our tree to show the same message.'

Mr Bear joined in the conversation. 'Now, here's the bit we need to think about. The Christingle orange has four sticks coming out of it, holding raisins, soft sweets and things like that, to represent the four seasons and the gifts that come to us from our world. We must hang things on our tree to show the same message.'

Teresa and Timothy were getting more and more into their theme. It wasn't such a bad idea after all.

'Chocolate and honey,' blurted out Teresa.

'Yorkshire pudding and roast potatoes,' went on Timothy.

'Colouring pencils and dancing shoes,' shouted Teresa.

'Grandpa,' whispered Timothy.

'Hold on,' said Dad. 'We'll have to get busy if we're to have everything in place. I'll see to the very top of the tree. There'll be no fairy or star at the top of our tree. A Christingle has a candle at the top of the orange, to show Jesus is the light of the world. I'm going to design a cardboard candle with a small electric lightbulb to be its flame. A real flame would be too dangerous in the branches of a tree.'

Over the next few days, every spare moment that the Bear family had was devoted to their Christingle tree.

On the eve of Christmas Eve, the church was packed for the Christingle service. It was already dark when the service started and the only lighting came from the hundreds of twinkling tiny points of light on the 18 trees. It was magical, even if it was quite hard to read the words on the carol sheet.

When the time came for his talk, the vicar said that he had arranged with Sparks for a special visual aid. At that moment, the lights of 17 trees went out and the lights of only one shone out. It was the Bears' Christingle tree. The vicar talked about Christingle, using the tree to help him. He even mentioned the importance of grandpas in God's scheme of things.

At the end of the service, each member of the congregation was given their own orange Christingle. To begin with, just the lights of the Christingle tree shone out but, as the vicar lit the candle of the nearest orange Christingle from his own, an increasing number of flames came to life in the church. Sparks switched on more and more of the Christmas tree lights until the whole place was aglow. When all was bright and all was still, the vicar spoke into the silence.

'May the light of Christ shine in our hearts so that we may be filled with his joy and his peace.' He paused and then went on. 'Let us go in the light of Christ, to bring light to all whom we meet.'

Timothy Bear really meant it as he joined with everyone else to say, 'Amen'.

Advent activity

Make your own picture of a Christingle. It will need careful colouring.

Prayer

Let us go in the light of Christ to bring light to all whom we meet with the help of God. Amen

— Day 24 —

Christmas Eve

... in which Timothy finds Christmas Eve passing slowly, Grandpa visits to brighten things up in more ways than one, and Timothy goes happily to sleep before the big day comes.

Timothy Bear woke up and it was Christmas Eve. Timothy, however, was wishing it was Christmas Day. Then there would be presents—there always had been. Then there would be fun and games—there always had been. Then there would be roast turkey for dinner and special puddings—there always had been. But it was Christmas Eve and time was already dragging. There was so little to do. Timothy slowly went downstairs.

'It's the last day of your Advent calendar,' Mum reminded him.

There was indeed just the one door left unopened, and it was the biggest door of all. When Timothy opened it, he saw the scene inside—the Bethlehem stable. It reminded Timothy of the final part of their nativity play at school. It also reminded Timothy of the model stable that Mrs Bear brought out every year and stood in the fireplace of their lounge. He hadn't really noticed it this year. It had become ordinary, worn, dull and just part of the Christmas furniture.

Time carried on dragging its feet, second by second. Breakfast was over and it was only nine o'clock. Why couldn't it be tomorrow? Then there would be excitement and things to do. For Mr and Mrs Bear,though, time was speeding by too fast. There was so much for them to do. Mind you, they did have time to work out the special Christmas Day television they would be watching.

Today, the plan was to have Christmas Eve lunch at the restaurant on the corner of their road. People just turned up, and at special times meals were cheaper than at other times. The Bears had not expected the long queues that greeted them. It would take over an hour before they were even seated.

'I can't possibly spare that amount of time,' sighed Mrs Bear.

'No room at the inn!' said Mr Bear. 'Where have I heard that before? We'll buy some sandwiches from the mini-market and eat them at home.'

They were just eating their sandwiches when the door bell rang. Mr Bear had spotted who was calling on them. 'Timothy, you go and answer the door.'

It was rare for Timothy to answer the door by himself but still he walked slowly. Would it never get dark?

'Grandpa!' exclaimed Timothy on opening the front door. Grandpa was delighted by his welcome. Timothy thought it was by far the best thing to have happened throughout this long day.

'I've an idea for that stable scene in your fireplace, if your mum agrees,' said Grandpa. 'And if she does agree, I could do with an electrician's mate to help me.'

Mrs Bear readily did agree and Timothy was only too willing to help.

Grandpa had bought a small bulb, a battery, some wire and an on–off switch. Timothy's smaller paws were just the right size to position the electrical circuit at the back of the stable and up into its roof. It took some time to get everything in position. At last it was time to test their workmanship. Grandpa turned off all the other lights in the lounge.

'It's dark!' gasped Timothy.

'You switch on the stable illumination,' offered Grandpa grandly.

The stable scene was transformed. There was only one small bulb but it made such a difference. The light lit up the baby in the manger especially. The shadows, too, made everything more real. The dull, worn-out scene had become bright and hopeful. Grandpa swiftly said his goodbyes. Timothy sat on in front of the stable.

Later, it was time for bed. Timothy never has any trouble about going to bed on Christmas Eve.

'Listen out for those reindeer bells,' said Teresa, tumbling up the stairs.

Timothy didn't go off to sleep immediately. Now he found that he didn't want the last few moments of Christmas Eve to pass too quickly. But in the end it wasn't reindeer bells he was trying to hear; it was more like the clip-clop of a little donkey and the tired bleating of sheep on a hillside. The sounds of four-legged animals became mingled with the gurgles and cries of a baby. And that spotlight, he wondered as he drifted between waking and sleeping—was it a golden beam lighting the stage at school, or was it Grandpa's light for their fireside model or, again, was it Timothy's own star to guide him to the great celebration of Christmas Day?

Advent activity

Spend some time thinking about the first Christmas. You might find pictures to help you or read the story together from a Bible, or from the Bible passages on pages 9–11.

Prayer

God our Father, we listen again to the story of Christmas and we are glad that Jesus has come to be our Saviour and our friend. We welcome him with our love. Amen

Decoration templates and instructions for Day 10

Mr Bear's equilateral triangle with all three sides 6cm long.

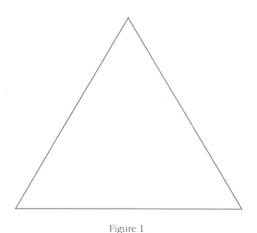

Figure 1

Cut out two equilateral triangles to make this six-pointed star.

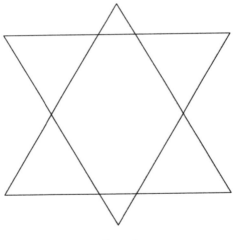

Figure 2

Draw round the equilateral triangle four times to make this larger equilateral triangle. Cut it out and fold along the thin lines to build up a pyramid. Tape the sides together.
Other mathematical decorations can be made. Colour helps to make the decorations sparkle.

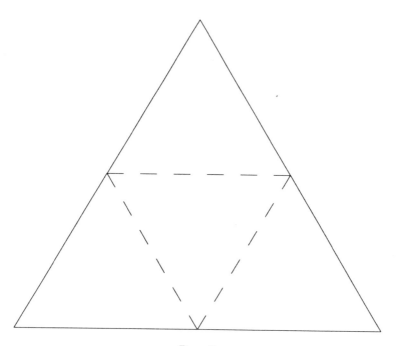

Figure 3

Also from BRF/Barnabas

The Barnabas
Read-Aloud Bible

24 five-minute stories for special days
and seasons of the year

Meg Wang

Illustrated by Heather Stuart

Perfect for bedtime or any time, this illustrated Bible for
children provides a short story for every day of the year.

ISBN 978 1 84101 708 2   £9.99
Available from your local Christian bookshop or, in case of difficulty, direct
from BRF using the order form on page 119.
You may also order from www.barnabasforchildren.org.uk.

The Shepherd's Song

Psalm 23 for children

Jan Godfrey
Illustrated by Honor Ayres

David knew that God was his good shepherd, giving him everything he needed, keeping him safe and showing him the right way to live. David's song can be our song too.

ISBN 978 1 84101 802 7   £6.99
Available from your local Christian bookshop or, in case of difficulty, direct from BRF using the order form on page 119.
You may also order from www.barnabasforchildren.org.uk.

The Secret of Happiness

The Sermon on the Mount for children

Jan Godfrey

Illustrated by Honor Ayres

Jesus knew the secret of happiness—but he didn't keep it to himself. He shared the secret with everyone he knew. We can learn Jesus' secret too.

ISBN 978 1 84101 801 0   £6.99
Available from your local Christian bookshop or, in case of difficulty, direct from BRF using the order form on page 119.
You may also order from www.barnabasforchildren.org.uk.

REF	TITLE	PRICE	QTY	TOTAL
708.2	The Barnabas Read-Aloud Bible	£9.99		
802 7	The Shepherd's Song	£6.99		
801 0	The Secret of Happiness	£6.99		

POSTAGE AND PACKING CHARGES

Order value	UK	Europe	Surface	Air Mail
£7.00 & under	£1.25	£3.00	£3.50	£5.50
£7.10–£30.00	£2.25	£5.50	£6.50	£10.00
Over £30.00	FREE	prices on request		

Postage and packing	
Donation	
TOTAL	

Name _____ Account Number _____

Address _____

_____ Postcode _____

Telephone Number_____

Email _____

Payment by: ❑ Cheque ❑ Mastercard ❑ Visa ❑ Postal Order ❑ Maestro

Card no ☐☐☐☐ ☐☐☐☐ ☐☐☐☐ ☐☐☐☐ ☐☐☐

Valid from ☐☐☐☐ Expires ☐☐☐☐ Issue no. ☐☐☐

Security code* ☐☐☐   *Last 3 digits on the reverse of the card.
ESSENTIAL IN ORDER TO PROCESS YOUR ORDER

Shaded boxes for
Maestro use only

Signature _____ Date _____

All orders must be accompanied by the appropriate payment.

Please send your completed order form to:
BRF, 15 The Chambers, Vineyard, Abingdon OX14 3FE
Tel. 01865 319700 / Fax. 01865 319701 Email: enquiries@brf.org.uk

❑ Please send me further information about BRF publications.

Available from your local Christian bookshop.   BRF is a Registered Charity

About
brf:

BRF is a registered charity and also a limited company, and has been in existence since 1922. Through all that we do—producing resources, providing training, working face-to-face with adults and children, and via the web—we work to resource individuals and church communities in their Christian discipleship through the Bible, prayer and worship.

Our Barnabas children's team works with primary schools and churches to help children under 11, and the adults who work with them, to explore Christianity creatively and to bring the Bible alive.

To find out more about BRF and its core activities and ministries, visit:

www.brf.org.uk
www.brfonline.org.uk
www.barnabasinschools.org.uk
www.barnabasinchurches.org.uk
www.messychurch.org.uk
www.foundations21.org.uk

If you have any questions about BRF and our work, please email us at

enquiries@brf.org.uk